ELIZABETH HOPKINSON is the author of *Asexual Fairy Tales*, which featured in the BBC's We Are Bradford project, and earned her a place in Wikipedia's Timeline of Asexual History.

Her short stories have appeared in *The Forgotten & the Fantastical* and *Dancing with Mr Darcy*, along with many other anthologies and magazines. Her story *A Short History of the Dream Library* won the James White Award.

Elizabeth has appeared at Leeds LGBT+ Literature Festival, Ilkley Literature Festival Fringe and Swanwick Writers' Summer School. She lives in Bradford with her husband, daughter and cat.

Find out more about Elizabeth at: www.elizabethhopkinson.uk

ANNA HOPKINSON is an illustration student at the University of Huddersfield. She is the illustrator of Asexual Fairy Tales.

To see more of her work, visit her Instagram: annahopkinson_art

CW00515731

Praise for *Asexual Fairy Tales*

"These Asexual Fairy Tales sound like old folk tales, perfect for reading out loud. More than just a retelling or adaptation, Elizabeth has succeeded in creating something new without losing that old-world storyteller feel."

— Jaylee James, editor of *Circuits and Slippers*

"Fairy tales are a part of every child's life. As we grow up, we learn mythology, history, and legends. Yet, for asexuals, the representation has always been rare to non-existent. What Elizabeth Hopkinson has done is brought aces to the forefront in these pieces of writing. It's an incredible and necessary thing! Everyone wants to see a character that is like themselves in what they read or watch, even when it comes to fairy tales. So what Elizabeth is doing here is greatly appreciated, and we wish her the very best!"

— Kelsey Lee, Social Media Director of AVEN

"If you love fairy tales but have seen enough retellings of *Beauty and the Beast* to last you a lifetime, try this. These twelve stories are drawn from a wide variety of sources, including a silent film. Some are straight retellings, others re-imaginings, and a third set originals by Elizabeth Hopkinson. The common thread, as per the title, is that they all feature asexual characters and explore what that is like in a society obsessed by sex. A gently enlightening read."

— L. Wade | Amazon review

"A good mixture of traditional and new stories, compellingly told. I also really liked the academic notes at the beginning of each story - I have several things to look up in more detail now."

— Jenn | Goodreads review

Asexual Myths & Tales

Elizabeth Hopkinson

SilverWood

Published in 2020 by SilverWood Books

SilverWood Books Ltd
14 Small Street, Bristol, BS1 1DE, United Kingdom
www.silverwoodbooks.co.uk

Copyright © Elizabeth Hopkinson 2020
Images © Anna Hopkinson 2020

ISBN 978-1-80042-023-6 (paperback)
ISBN 978-1-80042-024-3 (ebook)

British Library Cataloguing in Publication Data
A CIP catalogue record for this book is available from the British Library

Page design and typesetting by SilverWood Books

To Mum and Dad

Fairy Tale

She sleeps where the vines are unbroken
The vapours are at her command
She lives in a magical land

He comes to her home in the evening
The darkness has hidden his face
It is a mysterious place

When will she take the ring
And swear her love undying?
When will she take the light, and see
Immortal beauty flying?

She sleeps in glass
And walks in marble
Her footsteps echo through enchanted halls to the end of days
She hides in leaves
And in the tower of the poisoned rose
She's waiting for that kiss to wake her to a lover's gaze

She sings where there's no one to hear her
Her hair reaches down to the ground
Her voice doesn't make any sound

He waits at the foot of the tower
He waits in the depths of the earth
His promise will bring her to birth

When will she take the knife
And cut the cords that bind her?
When will she wake from dreams and see
The one who came to find her?

She sleeps in glass
And walks in marble
Her footsteps echo through enchanted halls to the end of days
She hides in leaves
And in the tower of the poisoned rose
She's waiting for that kiss to wake her to a lover's gaze

Song lyrics performed at the launch party for *Asexual Fairy Tales.*

Contents

	From the Author	11
1	The Little Mermaid Speaks	13
2	Cupid and Psyche	19
3	Snow White and Rose Red	29
4	Bisclavret	39
5	The True Love Knot	47
6	The Legend of Saint Wilgefortis	55
7	Princess Miao-shan	61
8	Attis and the Priests of Cybele	69
9	The Goddesses and the Boar	75
10	The Miracle of Marjatta	79
11	Clorinda the Knight	87
12	The Rose of the Alhambra	93
13	The Snow Maiden	105
14	Children of Wax	117
15	The Little White Bird	123
16	The Asexual Planet	133
17	A Wingless Wedding	139
	Story Sources and Further Reading	145
	Acknowledgements	149
	Supporters	151

From the Author

My 2019 book, *Asexual Fairy Tales*, was a deeply personal project for me. The tales in it had been on my mind and in my heart for years, long before I knew I was asexual. However, there were some tales I wanted to hold back to see if there was an opportunity for me to write a second book. Those tales are published here.

During the past year, I have also scoured the myths and tales of the world, looking for stories with an asexual theme, or which could be interpreted from an asexual perspective. I have discovered new stories I never knew existed, from many countries and cultures, which I believe have something to say about asexuality. I hope this excites you as much as it does me.

Again, I write this book from my own perspective as a heteroromantic, sex-repulsed asexual. When it comes to asexual tales, I have my own preoccupations - women in towers, eunuchs, parthenogenesis - which I know won't speak directly to everyone. But I do think this selection of stories reflects a little more of the spectrum than *Asexual Fairy Tales* did. I'll leave you to be the judge of that.

I exist and I am proud.

Elizabeth Hopkinson,
July 2020

The Little Mermaid Speaks

1

The Little Mermaid Speaks

Hans Christian Andersen's sexuality has been debated at length over the years. Some people think he was asexual (and biromantic). "The Little Mermaid" first appeared in English in Stories for the Household *(1889) and is a classic story of unrequited love. On rereading it for this collection, I was struck by the asexual symbolism to be found in it. The love of the Little Mermaid for the statue is reminiscent of Pygmalion (retold in* Asexual Fairy Tales*). The pain she feels when her tail is split into two legs speaks for itself.*

In my retelling, I have fused Andersen's story with the Classical Greek myth of Echo and Narcissus, another tale of unrequited, bodiless love and the loss of voice.

There are no books under the sea. All our stories are spoken ones, tales told from grandmother to granddaughter, from sister to sister. Tales of the mysterious world Above, with its gold and purple sky, its black ships and diamond icebergs, its scented flowers and flying birds. Tales with no beginning and no ending, like the sea itself.

In the palace of the King Above, there are many books. The Prince read me a tale from one of them about a man who fell in love with a marble statue and wished that it might come to life.

"How does he know?" I thought as he read. "This is my own story that he is telling back to me."

And yet it was not my story. When the statue in the tale came to life, it fell in love with the man and married him. The living person the statue became was just as the man had imagined. When my statue became a real person, nothing was as I had imagined. And I have no story to tell because I cannot speak.

I had a statue once, in my garden beneath the sea. I planted a weeping willow beside it, pink branches reaching down to kiss the blue sand. And I kissed my statue many times, there in my garden as round as the sun. When I saw the Prince on the deck of his ship, sixteen years old, with deep, black eyes, I thought my statue lived and breathed. When the storm broke his ship apart, I took him in my arms. I could have carried him down to the depths then to be with me forever. But not as a living man. He would have been as dead and still as a second statue. And what is a statue compared with a living soul?

So I laid him on the beach. I kissed his pale forehead and smoothed back his hair. And I hid behind the rocks when the maiden came walking from the convent garden and found the Prince upon the sand. I watched while he smiled on her and not on me. I watched until the sea foam dried upon my face. Until the sun scorched my hair.

Beneath the sea once more, I clung to my statue. But what had once brought me joy now brought only sorrow. The willow withered and the flowers ran to choking vines. I wanted my Prince. I wanted him so hard. Just to be near him, to have the right to love him. For him to smile at me with those deep, black eyes.

So, I sold my voice to the Sea Witch and went Above. I thought the Prince would see me and give me his soul, as I had given him my heart. But it was not like that. It was nothing like I had imagined when I kissed my statue beneath the sea. Needles and knives. Every step I took was needles and knives. When the Prince looked at me, he did not see a twin soul. He saw a "dear, good child", a girl whom he dressed as a page boy, to follow him on horseback across the kingdom.

"Why does he not see a woman?" I could not understand. The Sea Witch had promised that my beautiful form, my graceful walk and speaking eyes were enough to captivate a human heart. Day after day, I spoke to the Prince with mournful eyes. I danced as light as a soap bubble, more gracefully than any slave girl, and yet the Prince only saw his "dear little foundling". What did the slave girls know that I did not? What made their dance any different, free from needles and knives?

I could have been content with that life. Had I no need for the Prince to give his soul, things might have stayed that way. Every night,

I slept on a velvet cushion at the threshold to his chamber. Everywhere he travelled, he took me with him.

"You are the dearest of all to me," he would say. "For you are the most devoted and have the best heart."

And he would kiss my forehead, as I had once kissed his. Could this not be enough? Just to be near him, to have the right to love him. For him to smile at me with those deep, black eyes. But the Sea Witch had said we must become man and wife. One in body and in soul. Would that, too, feel like needles and knives?

And then he found her. The Princess who had been raised in a convent. She of the dark blue eyes, so like to mine. The one he believed had saved him.

"You will rejoice at my happiness, I know," he said to me, "for you are the most devoted to me of them all. You feel my joy."

I did indeed feel his joy. And in it, my own sorrow. I knew I must die for him. Oh, I would have died for him anyway! Had he told me to jump off a cliff, I would have jumped, buried myself and paid for the funeral. But this was final. This was the Sea Witch's price for not keeping to the letter of the bargain.

Tonight, the Prince took his new bride on board ship. Coloured lanterns were lit and the sailors danced to merry tunes. And I danced. Lighter and faster than ever before, whirling around and around on feet that trod upon needles and knives. Past midnight when the endless sky burned with stars. The Prince kissed his beautiful bride long and hard. She ran her hands through his raven hair, head thrown back. He carried her into the silken tent the sailors had erected, laying his bride upon cushions of gold and purple.

My sisters have given me a knife with which to kill the Prince. They bought it from the Sea Witch at the cost of their own hair. But as I draw aside the purple curtain and see the tangled limbs upon the velvet cushions, I know that I could never aspire to such a coupling as this. It is not in my nature. I was born with a tail, not two forked legs that feel to me like needles and knives. It is not the Prince's fault. I just wanted to be near him.

The night before we docked here, the Prince read me another story from his book. It told of a youth - Narcissus - who found his twin soul in the water. But the twin was merely his own reflection, and he wasted away for love of what he could not have. And all the while, he was watched by a maiden - Echo - whose curse was that she could not speak of her own accord, only repeat the last words spoken by others. And she wasted away for love of Narcissus, her bones hardening until she became a stone statue, which finally crumbled away, leaving nothing but an echo in the caverns.

I am both Narcissus and Echo, the Prince both my Echo and my Narcissus. Tonight I undergo my own metamorphosis, from maid to sea foam, from foam to cloud, from cloud to who knows what. The Prince will look into the water in vain, seeking the devoted page, the dear, good child, the mermaid who could have been his twin soul. The Prince will return to his silken tent and his Princess bride, but I will fly as vapour in the air, seeking out other "dear, good children" of this world. May they not be silent, as I was. May they have a voice, a story.

Cupid and Psyche

2

Cupid and Psyche

The tale of Cupid and Psyche appears in The Golden Ass *(also known as* Metamorphoses*), written in the late second century AD by Roman author Lucius Apuleius. Many scholars consider it to be the forerunner of "Beauty and the Beast", my favourite fairy tale. There are many similar stories around the world of a girl sacrificed to a so-called monster, who turns out to be anything but monstrous. Despite the fact that Cupid is also known as Eros, I have always thought of it as an asexual myth. It shows us the possibility of a relationship not cemented by animal desire, but by something delicate and beautiful.*

In The Language of Love *(2004), Megan Tresidder calls Cupid and Psyche a "unisexual couple", a perfect archetype of lovers "suspended in a kind of ethereal bliss".[1] To my mind, this makes them like that other perfectly suspended pair, the young lovers in John Keats' poem, "Ode to a Grecian Urn" (1819) which I highly recommend reading. It is with that urn that our story begins.*

I magine, if you can, a Grecian urn, a clay vase the colours of lamplight and darkness. Imagine you turn it in your hands and see, among the scenes of gods and mortals, two young lovers, androgynous, almost mirror images of one another. They are on the verge of kissing, yet they will never kiss, for they cannot move. They will forever be suspended in a moment of anticipation, untainted by knowledge and betrayal. Happy lovers! Who can they be? Let us imagine the urn can speak and tell their tale.

---

1 *The Language of Love* pp. 71, 73

There was a certain king and queen who had three daughters. The elder two were beautiful and charming in the ordinary way and soon gained princes for husbands. The youngest, however – whose name was Psyche – was so beautiful that the local people worshipped her as a goddess. They abandoned their worship of Venus, goddess of love and bringer of fertility, and gave their devotion to Psyche, a virgin and a mortal.

As a result, no prince would offer his hand to Psyche. No man could imagine the warmth of the marriage bed with Psyche. She was as a marble statue in a temple. The king and queen were covered with shame. No husband for their daughter? No grandchildren?

"It is a disgrace to have a barren line in our family," they said.

Worse still, the land itself grew barren. Crops failed, people began to starve, disease broke out. Soon the common folk were cursing Psyche.

"We thought she was our goddess," they said. "But look what has happened. What has she ever done for us? She is cursed."

"No, I am neither a goddess nor a curse," said Psyche. "I am merely myself." But no one listened to her.

The king and queen decided to consult the oracle of Apollo.

"Your daughter is an offence to Venus," the oracle said. "This barrenness shows the goddess's displeasure. To appease her, you must make a sacrifice. You must offer her as a bride to the One Who Dwells on the Mountain."

At this, Psyche's parents shuddered with horror. The mountain was the dwelling-place of a monster that neither gods nor men could resist. To make a girl his bride was to offer her to be devoured.

When they found the courage to tell Psyche, she shrugged, resigned.

"My life is miserable enough," she said. "Even to my own family, I am a stranger. Lead me to the mountain."

They dressed Psyche as a bride and led her in procession to the mountain, although it was more like a funeral procession than a bridal party. When they reached the summit, they left Psyche alone and returned home with tears in their eyes. Soon, the land returned to normal and the memory of Psyche faded from their minds. Only her sisters remembered, and wondered what had become of her.

*

Meanwhile, on the mountain, Psyche was left panting with fear. She closed her eyes and waited for the monster to come and devour her. Instead, a gentle breeze began to blow. It blew her to the other side of a mountain, where it lulled her to sleep.

When she awoke, she found herself in a grove of stately trees, in the midst of which was a fountain. Beyond this stood a palace, more magnificent than any she had seen.

Going inside, Psyche was awed by the marvels she saw. Gold pillars, painted frescoes depicting hunting scenes and the revels of nymphs and shepherds. Chamber after chamber opened out, filled with all manner of wonderful things. Elegant couches. Mosaic floors. A pool of clear water beneath a glass ceiling.

Another breeze blew past her shoulder and whispered in her ear, "We who walk invisible are at your service. We shall bathe you, dress you, wait on you at table. Whatever you wish to eat and drink will be brought to you. You are the mistress of this house."

Psyche was baffled. Where was the monster? Where were the horrors she had been told to expect? Here, all was beauty. The breezes bathed her in the crystal pool. They led her to a table, where they conjured food and wine from the air. Psyche was served from golden plates and from silver ewers. While she ate, the music of harp and lute played for her, and voices sang in high, clear harmony.

After this she was led to a bed of swansdown, where she fell asleep. But during the small hours, she awoke. There was a sound of footsteps. A shadow had entered the room. She felt the creak of the bed as someone lay down beside her. Psyche clutched the sheepskin coverlet about her and pulled her knees to her chin, her heart hammering. But the monster only sighed and lay still. Soon his slow breathing told Psyche he was asleep.

When morning light came, Psyche steeled herself to turn and take a first look at her husband. But he was gone. Only the indent in the feather bed showed he had been there at all.

"I was lucky to escape," she told herself. "But perhaps he will devour me tonight."

This thought was worse than if she had faced danger head-on. In vain, her invisible servants provided her with pastimes for the day. Musical instruments. Soft wools to weave. Scrolls of poetry and philosophy. All she could think of was the coming night.

When darkness fell, the monster came again. Again, he lay beside her in the bed. Again, she waited to be devoured. Again, nothing happened.

By the third night, she felt she must speak.

"What are you?" she said. "Show yourself to me. If you mean to devour me, do it now."

To her surprise, the voice that answered was not monstrous, but golden, a voice from the Garden of the Hesperides.

"Psyche, beloved Psyche, do not fear me. I do not wish to devour you. All I wish for is your love. But you may not see my face - that is forbidden. For I am a god and you are a mortal."

"Is your face so terrible, then?" Psyche said.

"You may find it terrible, you may find it beautiful," the god said. "I would rather you love me for what I am."

These words reminded Psyche of those she had spoken to her parents. From that time, she felt easier about her life in the palace and began to look forward to her husband's nightly visits. As each night passed, their talk became more tender. Sometimes, their fingertips would touch, or Psyche would feel warm breath and a feather-light kiss on her cheek. What need was there for more? What she had was perfection.

Yet a delicate bubble needs only a touch of rain to burst. One day, Psyche thought of her family, who supposed her devoured by a monster. Her parents had never understood her, but what of her two sisters? It was unfair to keep them in ignorance.

"Please may they come here, just for a day?" she asked her husband that night. "It would quiet their minds to know I am safe."

Reluctantly, the god agreed, and the next day, the winds blew Psyche's sisters over the mountain and into the enchanted valley. Psyche ran to meet them.

"Sister!" They hurried to embrace her. "We thought you were dead. We thought the monster had devoured you. But what is this place?"

Psyche showed them around her home with joy, and they marvelled at the splendours of the palace.

"But what of your husband?" they asked. "What is he like? Is he as hideous as everyone says?"

"No, he's not a monster at all," said Psyche. He's...lovely."

But her sisters persisted until Psyche was forced to confess that she had never seen him, as he always came at night and she was forbidden to look on his face.

"Then how do you know?" they said. "Oh, Psyche! What sort of a husband hides his face? You must listen to us – we have been married longer than you and know what's what. This so-called god is lulling you into a false sense of security, only to devour you when you least expect it."

Psyche protested, yet she remembered the shape of her husband's shadow in the dark. Huge, hunched shoulders of monstrous proportions. And had she not reached for him in the night and felt...what? Feathers? Fur?

"Take an oil lamp and a knife," her sisters said. "Then, when he is asleep, light the lamp and see for yourself what he is. If he is a monster, cut off his head."

Even after the winds had blown her sisters home again, their words echoed in Psyche's mind. She took a lamp and a knife, and waited till her husband slept. Then she uncovered the lamp and lifted it to behold her husband's face.

He was breathtaking.

No words in the mortal tongue could describe his beauty. Lamplight fell on a blushing cheek, ivory skin, golden ringlets. His chest was bare, the bones at his throat like two half-moons. And at his shoulders, two shining wings like the wings of swans. He was her perfect counterpart, the masculine to her feminine, and yet so androgynous, they could have been twins.

Psyche leaned nearer. As she did so, a drop of lamp oil fell on the sleeping god's shoulder. He awoke with a cry, spread his wings and flew out the window. The moment he did, the palace melted away to nothing, until Psyche was sitting in an empty valley of trees and grass.

The god fluttered in mid-air and looked down.

"Psyche, Psyche, why did you not trust me? I am Cupid, the son of Venus. My mother wanted me to punish you, but I fell in love with you. Now you have broken the prohibition, I must leave you forever."

And he flew away into the starry sky, leaving Psyche forlorn and weeping.

"Why did I do such a thing?" she asked herself. "What we had was perfect. Why did I feel the need to follow my sisters' counsel? There was no need for me to be like other brides. I had a god for a husband, and now I've lost him."

She lay on the ground, expecting to die. But dying of a broken heart is much harder than people expect. In time, Psyche got up and began to climb up the other side of the valley, in a direction she had never gone before.

In time she came to a temple of Venus. Knowing how the goddess hated her, Psyche trembled with fear. But she laid an offering on the altar, daring Venus to appear, steeling her will to confront her mother-in-law.

Venus appeared, her eyes flashing copper, her hair foaming like the sea.

"So, you dare to summon me, mortal? Do you think with one paltry offering you can make up for all the worship you stole from me? Or perhaps you are seeking your sick husband, laid up with the wound you so cruelly gave him." She tossed her head.

"It was a mistake, all a mistake," Psyche pleaded. "Please let me see my husband again. I will do anything."

"Anything?" A cruel smile came to the mouth of Venus. "In that case..." And she led Psyche into a storehouse of grain, kept to feed the sacrificial pigeons. "Separate all these grains one from the other, sorting out barley, millet, lentils, vetch, each in their own pile. Do it before sundown and you may see my son again."

When Venus left, Psyche sat in despair once more. Who could perform such an impossible task? Then she felt the breeze on her cheek, and a golden voice in her ear, saying,

"Look to the ants."

She looked towards her feet and saw an army of ants, marching in orderly lines. Carrying the grains high above their heads, they separated the crops into their respective piles. The task was finished well before sundown.

When Venus returned, she was furious.

"No mortal could do this. My faithless son has helped you! You must perform another task."

At dawn, Venus took Psyche to a riverbank. The river swelled with fearful rapids, and beyond it was a meadow full of golden rams.

"These are the rams of Ares. They are so fierce, they will trample anyone to death who enters the field. You must bring me a sample of wool from the fleece of each ram."

When Venus had gone, Psyche stood on the riverbank, trembling with fear, summoning the courage to brave its torrential waters. Then she felt the breeze on her cheek, and a golden voice in her ear, saying, "Listen to the river god."

Psyche bent down. The hissing of the reeds became a whispering voice.

"Wait until the noontide sun has driven the rams into the shade, and the naiads have sung my waters to calmness. Then you may cross in safety and glean the wool that has caught on the thorny hedges."

Psyche followed the river god's advice and returned with the golden wool. When Venus returned and saw what Psyche had done, she was furious.

"No mortal could do this. My faithless son has helped you again! But I will give you a task so deadly, I defy any mortal to complete it."

And so saying, she gave to Psyche a box.

"Take this box, and go to the Realm of the Dead. Ask Proserpine, Queen of the Underworld, for a sample of her beauty. Bring it to me here, in this box, before nightfall. I must adorn myself with it for the Feast of the Gods."

This time, Psyche was stunned.

"Go to the Realm of the Dead? So, Venus meant to kill me all along, and was only putting off the moment." She sighed. "And now it seems I must die by my own hand. Is that not what I have wished, ever since Cupid flew from me?"

She climbed to the top of a high tower, meaning to throw herself into the rocks below. But then she felt the breeze on her cheek, and a golden voice in her ear, saying, "Sweet Psyche, don't do it! There is a way into the Underworld without dying."

The voice explained how she might enter through a certain cave, pass by Cerberus the three-headed dog, and pay the ferryman, Charon, to take her over the River Styx.

"But do not eat the food of the Underworld. And do not look in the box, whatever you do," said the voice. "To look upon the beauty of Proserpine is certain death."

Psyche did as she was bid. She entered the cave, passed Cerberus and crossed the Styx, to stand before Pluto and Proserpine on their thrones. Proserpine graciously agreed to place a sample of her beauty into the box, and Psyche returned the way she had come, back to the Land of the Living.

But Venus did not come immediately. And the longer she waited, the more Psyche was tempted to look inside the box and see the beauty of Proserpine.

"I will just take one peep," she said.

One peep was all it took. She fell to the ground as one dead.

This deathly sacrifice to Venus released Cupid from his mother's prohibition. He flew like an arrow to Psyche's side. He found her, not dead, but only in a deathlike sleep.

"Ah, Psyche, now we have both suffered! But we will not be parted again."

He touched her lightly with one of his golden arrows and placed a tender kiss on Psyche's lips. She awoke from her sleep and there was Cupid, sitting by her side, more beautiful than ever.

"Beloved," she said, "forgive my folly. We are not as other couples and have no need to be. I see that now."

"Hush, darling," Cupid whispered.

He enfolded her in his wings, and together they flew to the palace of Jupiter. There, they drank a cup of divine ambrosia in the presence of the gods. Thus was their marriage sealed, and thus was Psyche made a goddess and the wife of Cupid for eternity.

Put down the Grecian Urn, for the tale is told. And yet the image remains. Two young lovers, eternally fresh and innocent, the mirror image of one another. Forever will she love and he be fair.

Snow White and Rose Red

3

Snow White and Rose Red

*Unlike most tales in the Grimms' collection, "Snow White and Rose Red"
was largely inspired by a literary fairy tale, "The Ungrateful Dwarf" by
Caroline Stahl (1776-1837). In Stahl's version, there is no bear. The sisters
overcome the Dwarf and live happily together, unmarried. Interestingly, Stahl
herself was unmarried and often changed the traditional lovers in her tales
for siblings. (Unlike Wilhelm Grimm, who was happily married to his next-
door neighbour Dörtchen Wild).*

*I decided to create my own, unique version of the tale. And I couldn't help
fusing it with another tale of sisters outwitting goblins, Christina Rossetti's
"Goblin Market" (1862). A bit ironic, since I find the poem disturbingly sexual,
but it seems to work here. In some cultures, the beard is a symbol of virility; to
repeatedly cut it is to break that power. The bear is a symbol of resurrection.
And my Snow White and Rose Red are asexual and demisexual, a little
spectrum of their own.*

*I don't have a sister, but I do have a daughter. And through these books
of tales, we are working together to fight the goblins.*

There is no friend like a sister. And there were no sisters like
Snow White and Rose Red.

They were named for the twin rose bushes that grew
outside their mother's cottage: one white and the other red. Snow
White was pale of skin, quiet and gentle. She was happy to walk alone
or to work in silence, deft of needle and knowledgeable of herb lore.
Rose Red was as dark and rosy as her namesake. She loved to dance
and sing, to run down the hillside for sheer freedom. It was she who
would brave the hiss of the goose to collect its eggs, or bring back the

stray goat from the mountainside. Together, the sisters were like two halves of one whole.

As children, they played together, walking hand in hand in the forest to gather berries, coaxing the hare and the trembling fawn to take food from their fingers. As young women, they dreamed together, spinning by the fireside along with their aged mother, as each took turns to read from the great illuminated book upon the shelf, filled with dark tales of a half-forgotten long ago.

"Do you think a prince will come to us?" Rose Red said, her hands clasped about her knees. "A noble prince and courteous, who would wear our favours in his helmet."

The mother smiled and shook her head, for they were poor peasants, and the only royalty they were likely to meet were the darting kingfisher and the bumbling queen bee.

Snow White said, "I wish he would not. My sister is enough for me. Who would be my companion if you left with a prince?"

"I will never leave you alone, sister," Rose Red said. Yet she thought she could love a man she had come to know as a friend, a prince who was both gentle and honourable.

Their mother called the two girls to her side.

"Listen closely, my girls," she said. "You may speak of princes but not all men are alike. In especial, beware the goblin men. They will tempt you with wicked fruit and lead you to make bargains you cannot keep."

The old woman's eyes misted, as though she saw things they did not. But the two girls shuddered as they spun the fine wool. The very idea of goblins was hateful to them.

One winter's evening, when snow lay thick on the ground and the window panes were feathered with frost, the three were spinning by the fire as usual. Suddenly, there came a knock at the cottage door.

"Hurry and open it, Rose Red," the mother said. "It may be some poor traveller, lost in the woods. What a dreadful night to be out in!"

When Rose Red opened the door, she gave a yelp of shock. For who should come in but a great, black bear, with a layer of snow coating his back? Stranger still, the Bear began to speak.

"Don't be afraid. I will do you no harm. I only wish to warm myself by the fire, for I am half-frozen."

A pet lamb at Snow White's feet whimpered, and Rose Red's pet dove fluttered against the bars of the cage. But the old mother, who was wise in many matters, got to her feet.

"Come in, sir. You are most welcome to our hearth." She moved the skeins of wool aside to make room on the rug. "Girls, take your brooms and brush the snow off this poor bear's coat so he doesn't leave puddles."

Giggling nervously, the girls did as they were told. The Bear shambled in and settled himself before the fire. Snow White soothed her lamb and went back to spinning. The mother returned to her place in the book.

The Bear's coat soon dried by the warm fire. It looked so furry that Rose Red couldn't resist stroking it. Soon, she persuaded Snow White to stroke the Bear too. He stretched his limbs and made a contented noise like the purring of an enormous cat.

When bedtime came, and the girls had climbed into the loft where they slept, the mother turned to the Bear.

"I will not ask your name, but you seem to me as one who has lost much. You may sleep here on the hearth if you like, safe from the cold and the evil weather."

"I am in your debt," the Bear replied.

So it was that, every evening that winter, the Bear would come to the cottage door and lie on the hearth before the fire until morning. With sunrise, he would shamble back into the forest, and the girls would not see him again until evening.

They soon lost all fear of him, and hugged and petted him as freely as if he were a cat. Snow White loved to stroke his thick, black fur and to comb the tangles out of it. She would bury her face in his neck, breathing in the scent of pine and mountain air. Rose Red loved to tease their guest, tickling his belly with sticks and cajoling him into games of rough and tumble. He would toss her between his paws until she screamed with laughter.

Then he would stretch himself on the hearth with a shuddering sigh and close his eyes.

When springtime came, the Bear announced that he must leave them.

"But why must you go, dear Bear?" said Snow White with tears in her eyes.

"Don't you love us any more?" demanded Rose Red. "I thought we were friends."

The Bear wrinkled his nose.

"Don't you fret, children. I'll be back next winter. But now the ground is thawing, and the season has come when goblin men emerge from their underground homes. I have long been at war with one of their kind and have yet found no way to break his power."

At this, Rose Red sniggered.

"What a tease you are, Bear! As if a great beast like you couldn't overpower a goblin."

But the mother gravely laid a hand upon the Bear's neck.

"Beware, my friend. The wiles of the goblins are without number."

The Bear nodded his great head.

"Until the snows fall again. I expect you two maids will have grown so much by then, I shan't recognise you. Be bold. Be vigilant."

As the Bear left the cottage, his pelt caught on a tiny nail, leaving a tuft of fur behind. Where it came away, Snow White fancied she saw a glimmer of gold. Then the Bear was gone, and she thought of it no more.

Springtime brought with it many chores. Seeds to be planted. Forgotten corners to sweep. Sometimes the girls remembered their absent friend, and sometimes they were too busy.

One day, Snow White and Rose Red had gone into the forest to pick wild garlic when they came upon a fallen tree with something bobbing up and down beside it. Drawing closer, they saw a goblin man, no taller than Rose Red's thigh. He had knobbly skin and a long, thin beard like an icicle jutting from his chin. His beard was stuck in a cleft, and he was tugging with all his might to get it out.

It was the first goblin the girls had met. He didn't seem crafty, but comical. First Rose Red and then Snow White began to laugh.

"Insolent daughters of men!" the Goblin cried. "Stop laughing and help me. Since sunup, I've been stuck here. I was trying to split the log for firewood and..."

He tugged his beard again and jumped about until his face was puce.

The two girls apologised and began to pull, but the beard was stuck fast. The Goblin swore and cursed.

"Sheep-brained dolts! Can you do no better than that?"

"We shan't help at all if you're going to be like that," said Rose Red, hands on hips.

At this, the Goblin softened his voice. "Help me, and I will give you a share of my treasure."

Rose Red's eyes lit at this last word, but Snow White seized her by the wrist.

"Remember Mother's words. We must not make bargains with goblin men." She turned to the Goblin. "A good deed is its own reward. I know how to free you now."

She took her needlework scissors from her apron pocket and snipped the ends off the Goblin's beard. But instead of being grateful, the Goblin roared with rage.

"What have you done? Fiend! How dare you cut my beard?"

With these words, he plucked a small, heavy purse from the cleft in the tree and rushed into the forest, howling as if they had cut off his leg.

The girls said nothing to their mother about the ungrateful Goblin. But some weeks later, they were going fishing. As they neared the pond, they saw what looked like a giant frog leaping about in the bulrushes. It was the same Goblin, with his beard entangled in his fishing line. A fish had taken the bait and was threatening to pull him into the water.

"Don't just stand there! Help me, you heartless mortals!"

"You don't deserve it, you know," said Snow White.

But the Goblin only howled, fit to bring the wolves running.

"Oh, give me the scissors," said Rose Red.

She snipped his beard until it broke free from the fishing line. The Goblin was furious.

"My beard! My beard! Have you any idea what you have done?"

With that, he fished a purse from among the reeds and he ran away, clinking and jingling as he went.

The weeks flew by, spring became summer. Their mother sent Snow White and Rose Red to the nearest town to buy ribbons and lace at the Midsummer Fair. Each had a coin in her purse, and they laughed and chattered as they walked along.

Their way led them over a common, scattered with large rocks. As they climbed the path, they saw an eagle swoop down and seize something in its talons. The thing screamed. It was the Goblin.

"Help me!" he yelled.

He looked so funny with his legs dangling in the air that the girls couldn't help but make it into a game. Each grabbed a leg and tugged hard until the eagle gave up the struggle. But as they pulled the goblin from the bird's talons, there came a loud cry. The last hairs of the Goblin's beard had been torn clean from his chin.

"You interfering idiots!" he shrieked. "Now look what you've done."

He picked up a sack from behind a rock, shouldered it and leapt down a hole in the earth.

The girls enjoyed themselves so much at the fair that they forgot all about the Goblin. But on the way home, they were walking back across the common when they saw something glittering in the grass. Precious stones of every colour lay scattered among the daisies. When the girls bent closer, they inhaled a delicious smell like the sweetest of summer fruits.

"The Goblin's treasure!" Snow White breathed.

"How beautiful it is!" Rose Red sighed.

"No, Rose Red. We mustn't take goblin gifts or taste their fruit."

"It's not a gift. It's payment," said Rose Red. "He owes us, after all we've done for him." Before Snow White could stop her, she reached out to touch it.

"Thieves!" A voice shrieked, "You cut off my beard so you could steal my treasure. But I will punish you yet."

The Goblin's face contorted with rage. He raised his hands, as if to cast a spell.

At that moment, there was a deafening roar. Out of the forest came a great black bear, its teeth bared in a snarl. It raised a paw to swipe at the Goblin.

"Spare me, my lord!" the Goblin snivelled. "Spare me and I will give you a share of my treasure. See these beautiful, precious stones! Smell their delightful scent! All this shall be yours..."

The Bear growled louder. "You dare offer me my own treasure?"

"No. Of course not, my lord. But look! Here are two delectable girls for you. Only think of the pleasure you would have in devouring them. Or..."

The Bear narrowed its eyes.

"Do not mistake me for one of your kind, Goblin. Even if I were so inclined, I would never treat women as property. Not everything is a transaction. But this is one payment long overdue."

The Bear swiped at the Goblin with its mighty paw. The Goblin fell and did not move again.

Snow White and Rose Red were paralysed with shock. But the Bear called out, "Snow White and Rose Red, don't you recognise me?"

It was their very own Bear! They ran to embrace him. But as they did, his coat of fur fell off. He stood up, and was transformed into a man, tall and slender, dressed from head to foot in cloth of gold.

"Do not fear," he said to the sisters. "I am still the friend you knew. I am a lord in Faerie, a skin-changer who can walk between worlds and live as either man or bear. I fell foul of the Goblin with a bargain that bound me to my bear's shape and allowed him to steal my treasure. But you, my dear friends, have set me free. The strength of a goblin lies in his beard, and when you cut it, I was freed to take my revenge. For this I must especially thank you, Snow White. It seems you are impervious to goblin wiles."

Snow White smiled and dropped a curtsey.

"But you, Rose Red," said the Bear Lord, "I must ask permission to court you and seek your hand in marriage. For I came to love you during the winter, and I think you love me."

Rose Red blushed and realised it was true. She could love a man she had come to know as a friend, a prince who was both gentle and honourable.

"But I cannot leave my sister alone," said Rose Red. "We made a promise to one another. And she loves you too, in her own way."

"As I love her," said the Bear Lord. "Dear sister Snow White, will you not come and live with us in Faerie? And your mother, too? My castle is very beautiful. We could all be very happy there."

Snow White's face fell.

"I did love you very much as a bear. And I think I could learn to love you as a friend and brother. But I cannot leave the home I love so well – the cottage and the herb garden, the lambs and the trembling fawns. I cannot leave the twin rose bushes to fade, untended."

The Bear Lord thought a while.

"I know what we must do," he said.

He made the slightest gesture with his hand. Something began to move inside the cast-off bearskin. Snow White went to look. There was the sweetest black bear cub she ever saw! She picked it up in her arms, stroked its warm fur and buried her face in its neck.

So Rose Red wed the Bear Lord. Each golden summer, they lived at his castle in Faerie. There, they planted a red and white rose bush to bloom outside their chamber window. And every winter, when the first snow fell, they would arrive out of the storm to knock at the cottage door. Snow White would let them in, and they would all sit around the hearth, where the old mother spun and a black bear lay sleeping before the fire.

Bisclavret

4

Bisclavret

This is one of my favourite stories. It is found in The Lais of Marie de France *(fl.1160-1215), a book of ballad-like poems from Brittany telling tales of knights and ladies. It is not necessarily an asexual story, although it is a tale of a man who forsakes his wife's bed and is seen by her as less than human. In some ways, it resembles "The Half-Marble Prince" (in* Asexual Fairy Tales*). It is a tale of someone who is not accepted in his original home, but finds a new home and family in what could be read as a homoromantic relationship.*

I have used "Bisclavret" in workshops to discuss guilty secrets and silent victims and the need to confront these issues. When it comes to accepting and revealing one's true identity, the tale of Bisclavret has much to teach us.

In Brittany, there was once a baron named Bisclavret.

To look at him, you would think he had everything he could wish for: riches, prowess, handsome looks, a beautiful wife and the favour of the King. But looks can be deceiving. Within the castle walls, relations between Bisclavret and his wife were not happy.

For some time now, Bisclavret had forsaken his wife's bed, and three nights out of every seven, he was nowhere to be found. This made the Wife deeply suspicious, as well as frustrated. At last she decided to confront her husband.

"If I ask you a question, will you answer me?" she said.

Bisclavret gently embraced his wife. "Of course. Ask away, dear heart."

"Tell me where it is you go, those nights you are away from me. I am afraid of your answer, yet I must know."

Bisclavret turned pale.

"Do not ask me that, my lady. Anything but that."

"So, it is as I feared. You have a lover," the Wife said.

"No." Bisclavret scowled. "Believe me, that is quite impossible."

"Then why do you not come to my bed? You are lying!" the Wife said.

However much Bisclavret pleaded with her, she insisted all the more strongly that he reveal the secret. In the end, Bisclavret could not refuse.

He drew a deep breath.

"Lady, I become a werewolf."

The Wife's eyes widened. Her veil quivered about the edges.

"It's true," Bisclavret said. "I become a werewolf and live in the deepest part of the forest, where I live off the small beasts I kill."

The Wife was horrified.

"And when you are a...werewolf," she swallowed, "do you go about the forest clothed or naked?"

"Lady," Bisclavret looked down, "I go about completely naked."

The Wife was disgusted. The thought of her husband, a respectable baron, going about the woods naked, like a wild beast! It made her sick.

"And where do you put your clothes while you are engaged in this... activity?"

"That I cannot tell you," Bisclavret said. "For if my clothes were to be discovered and removed, I would never be able to change back into a man. I would be forced to remain a wolf forever."

But the Wife would not let the matter rest. She pleaded and insisted until Bisclavret was forced to tell her.

"There is a ruined chapel just off the forest path. Inside it is a hollowed-out stone. I leave my clothes there."

The Wife questioned no more after this, but her heart towards Bisclavret was utterly changed. Before, she had been proud to have such a respected man for a husband. Now she was covered with shame. She thought of a neighbouring knight who was always flirting with her. Many a time, she had imagined his strong hands against her body. He was a real man, not like her freak of a husband! He would help her escape this humiliation.

Secretly, she sent him a message.

"I know you have always desired me. If you help me in this matter, I am yours, body and soul."

She told him of the chapel and the hidden clothes. The next time Bisclavret was away, he removed the clothes that would have made Bisclavret a man again.

Since Bisclavret was away from home so often, no one worried at first. When he did not return, folk began to question whether he had gone away for good. For a time, people searched and inquired after him, but nothing was ever heard. So, no one complained when the neighbouring knight moved in with Bisclavret's former wife and became her new husband. For surely she was now a widow, they said.

But Bisclavret was not dead. He was living the life of a wolf, deep in the forest. No one saw or heard from him for a full year, when the King decided to go hunting. The hounds took the scent of an unusual beast, which the King and his court pursued until late in the day. Eventually, they held the beast at bay. The huntsmen would have released the hounds and torn the beast to pieces. But to their astonishment, it ran up to the King's horse, took hold of the stirrup and kissed the King's foot. Human tears spilled from its eyes.

"Hold off the dogs!" cried the King. "This is an intelligent beast. Look, it pleads for mercy!"

The lords and huntsmen gathered around, and saw that it was true.

"I will hunt no more today," said the King. "I will take this beast home to my castle and place it under my protection."

From that day, the King kept Bisclavret as a pet. No one was allowed to hit or hurt him. All the lords and ladies were happy to stroke him. He was friendly and gentle, even to the smallest children. At night, he would sleep curled at the King's feet. Anywhere the King went, Bisclavret would go too. He would whine and cry if it looked like he would be left behind.

"And who could leave such a good boy?" the King would say, patting Bisclavret's fluffy head.

Some time later, the King celebrated a festival. All his knights and barons were required to attend court. Among those who came was the Knight who had married Bisclavret's wife and taken his lands. He never suspected the man he had wronged was so close by, in the form of the wolflike dog by the King's feet.

But Bisclavret knew the man instantly. The hackles rose on his back, and he began to growl. With a hideous snarl, he hurled himself at the Knight, bringing him to the ground. The King had to threaten Bisclavret with a stick before he would release the man.

Twice more that day, Bisclavret tried to bite the man. The servants had to take him to the kitchens and tie him up until the feast was over.

"I don't understand it," the King said. "He's normally so gentle." He thought for a while. "Perhaps you look like someone who harmed him before."

"Maybe," said the Knight, reluctantly. "But it wasn't me. I never saw the beast before."

Needless to say, when the feast was over, this Knight was the very first to leave. He couldn't wait to get back home.

More time passed, and the King made a progress of his lands. One of the places he stopped was the forest region where he had gone hunting and first discovered Bisclavret.

When Bisclavret's ex-wife heard that the King was in the neighbourhood, she put on her finest clothes and set out to present him with an expensive gift. Since her husband had made such a fool of himself at the festival - incompetent man! - it was up to her to set things right.

The moment she came into the King's presence, Bisclavret leapt through the air with a snarl. Before anyone could stop him, he had bitten the nose clean off the lady's face!

What a commotion! The whole court was in uproar. Servants and surgeons, knights and ladies, everyone was clamouring for the King's attention.

"You must have him put down! I demand it!" the Wife hollered.

"Madam, will you keep still while I dress your wounds?" the Surgeon said.

"If Fluffy bit you, it's your fault!" said the King. "I'd sooner die myself than have him put down."

"Diplomacy, Your Majesty, please!" begged the Lord Chancellor.

At last, an old and very wise courtier called for silence.

"Your Majesty," he said, "this beast has lived with you a long time, and every single one of us has been with him at close quarters. During all this time, he has been gentle and docile. The only people he has ever attacked are this lady and her husband. Can that be a coincidence?" He approached the King and lowered his voice. "This is the wife of your baron Bisclavret, who disappeared in mysterious circumstances. I do not trust her, my liege."

So, the King had the Wife taken away for questioning. And whatever form that questioning took, it soon got her to confess. She revealed the truth about her former husband – how she had betrayed him and taken his clothes, what had become of him and where he went. As Bisclavret had not been seen since his transformation, she was sure he and the beast were one and the same.

When the King heard this, he was astonished and horrified.

"Seek out this chapel and find Bisclavret's clothes immediately," he said.

Riders were dispatched and soon returned with the clothes. But when they were placed before Bisclavret, he would not even look at them.

Then the wise man spoke up once more.

"Your Majesty, you are not doing this properly. Put yourself in Bisclavret's position. Think of the embarrassment and humiliation it would bring him to have everyone watch his transformation.

"Now, why not do as I suggest? Take Bisclavret into your bedchamber, bring him the clothes and shut the door behind him. Give him time. It is the least you can do."

"Of course, you are right," said the King.

He did as the wise old man suggested, and waited outside the door for a decent length of time. Then he opened the door. Bisclavret was sleeping on the King's bed, fully clothed and human once more.

With a cry of joy, the King ran to embrace his friend and kissed him many times.

"Bisclavret! What a happy day this is!"

The King wasted no time in restoring to Bisclavret his land and titles. However, Bisclavret chose to spend his time at court. There he could be close to his friend the King, who loved him so dearly.

The wicked Wife and her Knight were banished from the kingdom of Brittany forever. And, if you will believe it, the descendants of that pair have all been born without noses, to this very day.

The True Love Knot

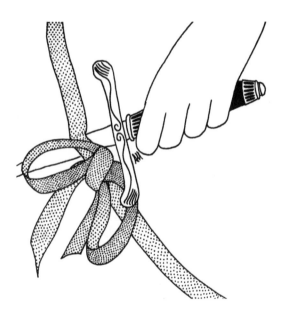

5

The True Love Knot

This is one of my early stories, which first appeared in My True Love Sent
to Me *(2009) under the title* Nine Pipers Piping. *It is an Arthurian story
inspired by the writing of Marie de France and her near contemporary,
Chrétien de Troyes (c.1170-82). It deals with the difficulties of distinguishing
between brotherly love and romantic love, and coping with marriage as an
asexual. I wrote this when I was still wrestling with my identity, and I think
the conclusion is closer to a demisexual experience than that of the romantic
asexual I turned out to be.*

*It's no coincidence that Sir Lancelot, who acts as agony uncle in this tale,
is the father of Sir Galahad and the unrequited love of* The Lady of Shallot,
two of my asexual icons.

In the days of Arthur, there was once a great tournament at Tenebroc
to celebrate the wedding of one of his noble knights. It was a
magnificent spectacle, such as had never been seen in those parts.
Before a lance was couched or a horse was spurred, the festivities had
already gone on for a fortnight, with torches burning late into the night
and many wonderful entertainments. Tumblers and jugglers, singers
and storytellers and musicians of all kinds had contributed to the
merrymaking. But most beloved by the knights and nobles of Arthur's
hall had been a troupe of nine pipers, all brothers of one house, who
made music on pipes from the weighty bass to the delicate soprano no
thicker than a straw; and their younger sister, Fauve, who danced to their
music, accompanied by her tabor.

Not only among the nobles were these minstrels beloved. Living
in the town of Tenebroc was a swordsmith by the name of Kerrin who

had loved Fauve for several years. (For the minstrels often returned for Arthur's revels and Kerrin was valued at the tournaments for his skill in all kinds of metalwork.) It happened at this time that King Arthur, who was by no means ungenerous, had offered a purse of money to anyone, high or low, who celebrated his marriage at the time of the tournament, and so participated in the joy of the court.

Kerrin therefore summoned the courage, on the eve of the tournament, to go to Fauve and her brothers, and ask for her hand. He arrived as the minstrels were loading their instruments into their cart, along with the gifts of coin, furs and fine woollen cloth, which were Arthur's reward.

"My good men all," Kerrin began. The brothers ceased their packing and turned to him with friendly faces. Fauve glanced at him shyly from behind the hanging pipes. "Our friendship has lasted some time and you can guess the reason for my visit tonight. I am a respected and valued craftsman in this town and, with the King's purse, I could provide your sister with a comfortable life. She knows I have loved her deeply these past years and I would take great care of her. I beg that she might become my wife."

Fauve's eldest brother was overjoyed and was quick to exchange gifts with Kerrin. Among the nine, there were many smiles, as most had secretly longed for this day. But there were also tears, not least from Fauve herself. For, while she was fond of Kerrin and knew he loved her dearly, he did not seem as handsome and talented as her brothers. The ringing blows of metal against metal could never compete with the melodious sound of the pipes. Particularly from her youngest brother she feared to part, he who had been her bosom companion from cradle days. So, while the swordsmith and the pipers drank together, she snuggled to her youngest brother's side and whispered to him of her trepidation.

"I will miss you too, little sister, more than I care to say," he replied. "But, since we cannot put off this day, I will give a gift to help you. Take it and you will never truly be parted from us so long as you live."

So saying, he unfastened the ribbon from Fauve's tabor and tied it as a sash around her waist – in the bare, narrow strip between her skirt and her stays – twisting and crossing it in an endless knot that none but his hands could undo. Neither Kerrin nor the other brothers saw what he did. Gradually, sleep came upon the party and they all slumbered until the morning, all except Fauve, who was restless and wakeful all night.

In the morning they presented themselves, with many other couples, before Arthur's throne, and were glad to receive the gift he had so graciously promised. When the priest had blessed them, Kerrin and the pipers celebrated a little more. Meanwhile, the fields between Tenebroc and Evroic, shook with the thunder of hooves, and many mighty shields were splintered. Arthur's knights won the opening day of the tournament, and Kerrin carried his new wife home to the sound of resounding cheers.

But, as he laid her gently on the bed, Fauve slipped into a trance. Her eyes remained closed like one in the deepest sleep. Vainly Kerrin tried to entice her with soft words of love and tender kisses; she was beyond his reach. Disappointed, he lay on the bed beside her and drifted into an unhappy sleep of his own.

The following day, Fauve awoke refreshed and smiling. She had had a most pleasant and vivid dream, which she treasured in her heart. But Kerrin was sullen and restive as he went about his work. Although Fauve worked for most of the day preparing the finest meal she knew, when Kerrin came to eat it there were no compliments. He seemed eager only for night to fall again.

There were no cheers in Tenebroc that evening, for Arthur's knights had fared badly, and it was in silence that Fauve and Kerrin went to the little attic room they shared. The instant Fauve's head touched the pillow, she fell once more into a deep trance. This time, Kerrin called to her and gently shook his wife, but to no avail, and he was forced to sleep coldly beside her.

The third day of Fauve and Kerrin's married life was much like the second. At first, Fauve was happy and contented, refreshed by her dreams. But, as the day wore on, the frustration of Kerrin marred her happiness and she could not understand how she had offended him. After all, she had cleaned and cooked and sewed as every good wife should. Surely he could not be ashamed of her appearance; she kept herself immaculate. Her confusion seemed to extend into the streets around, for the outcome of the day's jousting had been uncertain, and the noble visitors awaited Arthur's decision on the fourth day.

That night, as Kerrin lay miserably beside his entranced wife, he noticed the knotted sash around her waist. Eagerly, he tried to untie it, that he might at least catch a glimpse of her shapely body. But it was too tight and too intricate, and he could not manage it at all. In sheer annoyance, he ran to fetch a silver dagger from his workshop, with which to slice the offending ribbon. At the touch of silver, the ribbon began to sing, with a music Kerrin recognised. He took it in hand to slash it. But the knife slipped and cut his finger. Tears of pain and annoyance wet Kerrin's eyes, but at the sight of Fauve's sleeping figure, they softened and turned to tears of love before he angrily wiped them away.

On the fourth and final day of the tournament, Kerrin was disturbed early by a knocking at the door. One of the squires had come on behalf of his master to request his expertise in the field of weaponry. Glad of the change, Kerrin gathered his tools and set off. Fauve went with him, although there was little conversation between them.

Now the squire's master turned out to be none other than the mighty Sir Lancelot du Lac, who had taken as many wounds on the field of love as on the field of battle and, above all men, knew what it was to be torn in two for the sake of love and loyalty. In a short time, he perceived Kerrin's irritability and Fauve's silent tears and with all courtesy discreetly drew the swordsmith into conversation. It was not long before Kerrin confessed the disappointment of Fauve's nightly trances and the betrayal of the endless knot.

Sir Lancelot considered. "If you would allow me but a few moments' conversation with your wife, I may be able to help you. It would be the least I could do in return for your services."

Touched by the knight's generosity, Kerrin assented. Sir Lancelot drew Fauve gently aside and showed her the picture of Queen Guinevere on his shield.

"Here is one I greatly love," he said, "and yet with her I can never truly share happiness. How terrible is such a pain! I would not wish it on anyone alive."

At his words, the tears flowed faster down Fauve's cheeks, and her hand strayed to the true love knot at her waist.

"How terrible indeed," she repeated.

"Now tell me where you go at night, my dear," said Sir Lancelot. For he had seen True Love Knots before and knew of their power.

"To my brothers, the pipers," she said. "They call for me to come. We play and dance together, as we have done these many years, and when the sun rises, they bring me back to my husband. So I keep my love for all of them. But I fear that Kerrin does not love me as he claimed. I have tried to please him but he only grows colder. Would that the night were endless, for my days have become miserable."

She wept again. Sir Lancelot pitied her, but he knew too well the only solution to her problems.

"When the tournament is at its height, you must go to the stream that lies just beyond the town. Take your husband's silver dagger, cut the ribbon and throw it into the stream, and your married life will be a happy one."

"Never!" cried Fauve, for the thought of cutting this last tie with her brothers was unthinkable. But, after Sir Lancelot and his squire had left for the tournament, she thought better of it. Though she trembled as she did so, at mid-morning she crept out, dagger in hand, to the stream the knight had spoken of.

At the first touch of silver, the ribbon began to sing. Fauve knew the melody instantly for the song her brothers played at the close of every performance. Her hand shook and the knife vibrated; the music seemed to pierce her soul. But the knife did not turn aside for Fauve. It sliced the ribbon cleanly, which fell into the stream. It bobbed and circled for a while before drifting slowly out of sight on the current. The music fell silent. Fauve sobbed all the way home and went directly to bed, her head aching with tears. Surely, the knight must be wrong. This could never be the path to a happy marriage.

The tournament – as fame later told – came to a spectacular climax. By virtue of amazing feats of horsemanship, Arthur's knights were victorious, and Sir Lancelot himself was only outdone by the knight whose wedding celebration it had been. The knights caroused and made merry until late into the night, and in the morning when it was time to go, Lancelot had quite forgotten the young couple of the day before.

But, in the swordsmith's cottage, as the sun warmed the chamber, Fauve woke from a dream quite unlike the others. Her brothers had failed to call her, but Kerrin had been there. He had been unusually handsome and charming, and possessed of something strange and wonderful. As she opened her eyes, she heard the song again, as it had rung from the blade of the knife. She went downstairs. Kerrin - who for some reason had let her sleep late - was working at his forge. And, not only the silver dagger, but the tongs and the irons and the blades of the newly forged swords, sang with the melody of her brothers' song. Kerrin turned and smiled at her, and she knew that the dream had been no dream at all.

Many months later, as Sir Lancelot was about his errantry, he stopped by the banks of a gently flowing river. There, as he stopped to water his horse, he recognised Fauve's ribbon, caught against a rock. It was neither cut nor torn but completely whole, and shining with colour in the afternoon sun. With a gloved hand, Lancelot reached into the water and took it. At that moment, he heard the rumbling of cart wheels and saw in the distance the nine travelling pipers driving back towards Tenebroc.

The Legend of Saint Wilgefortis

6

The Legend of Saint Wilgefortis

A medieval saint's life, "The Legend of Saint Wilgefortis" appears in the 1815 edition of Grimm's Fairy Tales as "Die heilige Frau Kummernis". The saint is known by many names in different lands, including Uncumber, Kummernis, Liberata and Dignefortis.

Veneration of Saint Wilgefortis spread in the fifteenth and sixteenth centuries, and was said to grant an anxiety-free death. She seems to be a wholly fictitious saint; indeed some scholars believe her legend arose from the misinterpretation of early medieval portrayals of Christ on the cross wearing long robes, which later worshippers mistook for women's clothes, and so thought they were looking at a bearded woman.

However, there is something about Wilgefortis's story that transcends "reality". Although she was removed from the official Vatican calendar in 1969, she has been taken up by the Queer community as a patron saint of many identities, including intersex, transgender and asexual.

Long, long ago – so the story goes – there lived a princess named Wilgefortis, daughter to the King of Portugal. And as with so many royal daughters, her father arranged for her a marriage. She was to wed the King of Sicily, and so become a peace-weaver.

It was a noble calling, and one to which Wilgefortis had been brought up, but everything in her being was repelled by the idea of being the king's wife. She did not know the man. Moreover, he was a pagan like her father, while she secretly followed the Christian religion. And most of all, the idea of sharing the king's bed filled her with a nameless horror.

"You will grow used to it," her mother said.

"I'll teach you what to do. You'll enjoy it," said her waiting woman.

But it was all in vain. The more they tried to help her, the more miserable Wilgefortis became.

Worse still, it seemed the Sicilian king was enamoured with her. He sent her poetry, which the scholars of her father's court blushed to translate, all about coming into the fragrant garden and lying under the date-laden palms. All Wilgefortis could see of her future was an eternity of torture, night after endless night.

In desperation, Wilgefortis prayed for a way out.

"Anything, Lord. Anything at all. Just stop the wedding."

When she awoke the next day, a most miraculous thing had happened.

The undermaid noticed it first. She parted the silk curtains around Wilgefortis' bed and screamed. Soon, all the ladies-in-waiting came running. When Wilgefortis demanded to know what was wrong, they produced a bronze mirror. There in her reflection was the answer to her prayer.

She had grown a beard.

Not just a scanty bit of stubble, either. A full beard, covering her chest, as bushy as you like. Wilgefortis regarded the bearded lady in the mirror with calm satisfaction. Within the castle of the soul there is a gallery of selves, so the scholars say. It seemed to Wilgefortis that an alternative self had taken up residence in her face, giving her former self leave to retreat. All in all, she was pleased with what she saw.

Not so the waiting women. They tried everything to get rid of that beard. They snipped and they shaved, they applied creams and ointments. And when that failed, they tried holy water, charms, incantations, prayers... Nothing worked. The moment it was cut, the beard grew back as bushy as before.

Needless to say, the King of Sicily was horrified by this new development, and took back his betrothal vows. Wilgefortis' prayer had been answered.

The king her father could scarcely contain his disgust at the sight of a bearded daughter.

"Begone from me! You are an abomination!" he said.

"I am the same person I always was," Wilgefortis replied. "But if you wish me gone from your sight, I would gladly become a Christian nun. That life would suit me, I think."

This put the king into an even greater rage.

"Not only an abomination, but a Christian! A betrayer of your people's faith! This will end badly for you."

Tragic to relate, things did end badly for Wilgefortis. Her father was so enraged that he had her crucified, and she became a martyr of the church.

But her story does not end there. After her death, many people came to pray before her image. The tale goes that a fiddler, poor and destitute, knelt before her statue playing his fiddle. In compassion, the saint gave him one of her golden boots. But when the elders of the town saw a beggar in possession of such a treasure, they arrested him for a thief. In vain, he protested that St Wilgefortis had gifted it to him. The magistrates insisted he must hang.

"Have you any last requests?" they asked the fiddler.

"Yes," said he, "I would like to play my fiddle before St Wilgefortis one last time. For she alone in this world was kind to me. She understands what it is to be an outcast and falsely accused."

The fiddler's request was granted. Once more, he knelt before the statue and prayed. And there, in sight of the clergy, the magistrate and all the elders of the town, St Wilgefortis kicked off her other boot in the fiddler's direction. Thus was his innocence proved.

To this day, statues of St Wilgefortis have only one boot, while the fiddler kneels beside her, making his music. And Wilgefortis is held in honour by all who know what it is to have a gallery of selves within their soul.

Princess Miao-shan

7

Princess Miao-shan

I first read this story in The Chinese Wonder Book *(1919) by Norman Hinsdale Pitman. It is actually an origin story for Guanyin, the Buddhist bodhisattva of compassion, whom the Jesuits called the Goddess of Mercy, comparing her with the Virgin Mary. Her story compares nicely with that of Wilgefortis, showing how a meaningful tale can appear time and again, across cultures and religions.*

Interestingly, Guanyin (who is venerated by many names in many lands) is depicted in both female and male manifestations, and is believed by some to be androgynous or without gender.

There was once a princess, Miao-shan by name, who was beautiful, compassionate and intelligent.

Every day, she spent time alone in her chamber, reading and studying many books. She especially loved the Scriptures of the Buddha, poetry and philosophy. And every day, she went out among the less fortunate, listening to their troubles and doing what she could to ease them. For this reason, she was beloved by the common people, as well as by her own mother and sisters.

Her father the King also loved her, and had great plans for her life. As the wisest person in the kingdom, he planned that she would be his heir, ruling jointly with the husband he had assigned for her. But when he told Miao-shan of this plan, she was not happy.

"Honoured Father, why did you not consult me before planning my marriage? I have no desire for a husband. You know that among the priests there are those who say I have lived on this earth before, as a prince. I feel in my heart that it is so. There is a part of my soul that is neither male nor female, but something beyond either. A husband could not comprehend that.

"And, Honoured Father, you must know that I do not enjoy the pomp of court life. I prefer to spend my time in the marketplace and the homes of our people. My dearest wish is to please the Buddha by becoming a nun and joining a convent. For my marriage can do nothing to ease human suffering, but serving as a nun might."

At this, the King was very angry.

"Is this how you show your filial piety? You will marry the prince I have chosen for you, and that is an end to it."

Miao-shan's mother and sisters also pleaded with the King to see reason.

"Do you not remember the night she was conceived?" said the Queen. "I told you that I dreamt I swallowed the moon. This child is a gift to us from heaven. Fate has made her unique. She was not born for an ordinary life."

This made the King more furious than ever.

"Fine!" he said. "If you all think Miao-shan is so special, she shall go to the convent. She shall go to the Cloister of the White Sparrow, the strictest convent in the land." He glared at Miao-shan. "I shall make sure there is no special treatment for you on account of your rank. You will suffer every privation there is. Then we will see if you do not come crawling back, begging for marriage."

So, Miao-shan set out for the Cloister of the White Sparrow, and knocked at the gates. She was dressed in plain garments, but the abbess had been told to expect the runaway princess, and knew her at once.

"No room!" she said, when Miao-shan announced her desire to become a nun. "All our cells are full. We can take no new postulants at this time."

"Please," said Miao-shan, "I have come a long way to join you. I will do any menial task you ask of me. Only let me stay."

"Any task?" The abbess's eyes glittered. She had put up with her share of noblewomen supposedly renouncing the world, only to expect a quiet and easy life. "Well, perhaps we have room for a lay sister. You'll have to work hard, though. No special treatment for you."

"I should not wish it," Miao-shan said.

"Then come in," said the abbess, with a satisfied grin.

*

Although Miao-Shan had been promised no special treatment, the abbess made sure she was treated worse than any other sister in the convent. There was no rest for her. Day and night, the sisters set her the hardest and most degrading tasks. She must trudge up and down the hill three times a day to fetch water from the well, and must carry the heavy buckets alone. She must gather firewood in the nearby forest, even at dusk, although that forest was a well-known haunt of beasts and demons.

Miao-shan was determined not to complain, but to treat her fellow nuns as true sisters. She meditated as she trudged to and fro, freeing her mind from the daily world. She paid back the nuns' harsh words with kindness. She drew strength from the shade of trees, the blooming of delicate flowers and the song of birds. Thus, the abbess often found Miao-shan serene and smiling, when she would have expected tears of rage.

One day, Miao-shan had been sent to gather brushwood in the forest as usual. The repetitive work soon calmed her into meditation, and she didn't notice a tiger prowling towards her through the undergrowth until the beast was almost upon her. Her heart hammered at the sight of its teeth. But the tiger gently nuzzled her hand and began to purr like a kitten. Miao-shan stroked the flames of its fur. The tiger rolled on its back, exposing its soft belly.

"Sister Tiger, I wish I could play with you. But I have firewood to gather," Miao-shan said. "The abbess will be angry if I do not return on time."

At her words, the tiger bounded into the bush and came back with a bundle of firewood in its mouth. It went here and there, bringing more and more wood while Miao-Shan watched in amazement. Her work was soon done, and Miao-shan returned to the Cloister of the White Sparrow happier than usual, because she had found a friend.

When next the abbess sent her to the forest, she found a whole host of animals gathering wood under the supervision of the friendly tiger. Boars carried loads on their tusks, monkeys broke off the highest twigs, and even roosters scratched the forest floor for dead leaves. In a short time, they had gathered enough wood to supply the convent for the next six months! The abbess was baffled on Miao-Shan's return but Miao-shan said nothing. She hugged her new friendship tight inside her. Surely the Scriptures spoke truly that all things have the Buddha-nature within them!

Another time, Miao-shan went to draw water from the well, only to find a large, blue dragon blocking her path. Miao-Shan was astonished!

"Lord Dragon, to what do I owe the honour?" she said.

The dragon said nothing, but twisting its sinuous body, it flew into the air and up the hill, back towards the convent. Miao-shan ran after it. By the time she reached the courtyard, the dragon was gone. But in the centre of the courtyard stood a little building that had never been there before. It was a well. It had four sides with four arches. And above the west-facing arch was a tablet bearing the words: *In Honour of Miao-shan the Faithful.*

Miao-shan was awestruck. Not only would she never have to go down the hill for water again, but a dragon-lord had honoured her with his gift!

For a time, the nuns were also dumbstruck by the appearance of the well, and treated Miao-shan with a new reverence. But it wasn't long before they forgot the miracle and went back to their old ways of scolding and name-calling.

Meanwhile, Miao-Shan's father was losing patience. He had been sure the harsh regime of the convent would be enough to break his daughter, and that she would have come home weeping by now, begging for marriage.

"Enough of this folly!" he said. "General! Send troops to the Cloister of the White Sparrow and set fire to it. Keep the flames burning until the princess comes out and surrenders herself."

In the dark of night, the nuns were disturbed from their prayers by a crackling sound and a smell of smoke. They ran from their cells, wide-eyed and shouting all at once. The roof of the convent was ablaze. Stationed around the perimeter were soldiers with flaming arrows.

"Surrender the Princess Miao-shan at once!" yelled the Captain of the Guard.

"Princess?" Most of the nuns were astonished. "That little good-for-nothing?"

"Yes, it's true," Miao-shan admitted. "I came here hoping to escape an arranged marriage. But it seems my father will not relent after all."

"I should have known you would bring us ill luck," one of the nuns said. And the others joined in. "See what you've brought us to. We're all going to die!"

"We are not all going to die," said Miao-shan. "Nor shall the convent be destroyed."

And pressing her forehead to the ground, she prayed fervently.

Within moments, a fresh breeze began to blow. Large raindrops splashed to earth. Soon, there was a downpour worthy of the monsoon season. The dragon-lord had answered Miao-shan's call!

As soon as the fire was out, the rain stopped. Miao-shan got to her feet.

"I shall not bring further trouble to your door, sisters. I will surrender myself to my father's troops. Please pray for me."

The nuns stood in silence. The girl they had so abused had saved their lives.

When Miao-shan once more stood before her father, there was no mercy in his eyes.

"You have one last chance," he said. "Will you accept this marriage?"

"I will not," said Miao-shan. "The gods have made me what I am, and I shall not pretend to be anything else."

"Then I have no choice but to put you to death. Take her away!"

And though her mother and sisters begged and pleaded, the king would not listen. Poor Miao-shan was taken to a place of execution and killed like a common criminal.

She woke to the sound of a tiger's purr. There beside her was her friend from the forest, only transfigured. The tiger was huge and white, and a golden glow shone from her fur. All else was darkness.

"This is the realm of the dead, my princess. I have come to escort you to King Yama to be judged, because you disobeyed your parent. But do not fear." The tiger nuzzled Miao-shan's hand. "I do not think he will detain you long."

The tiger spoke truly. As they walked through the ravaged wastes of the underworld, flowers sprang up at Miao-shan's feet. Dead trees blossomed and birds began to sing. By the time she stood before Yama's throne, she may as well have been standing in paradise.

Yama's crimson face scowled, his eyes bulged under his bushy eyebrows.

"What are you doing in this place, woman of virtue?" he cried. "Depart this instant before you destroy my realm. This is a place of punishment, not a pleasure garden. You should be feasting on the peaches of immortality in the palace of the Jade Emperor."

And instantly, Miao-shan flew away to the highest heaven. There she was welcomed as a divinity on account of her virtuous life and given a new name: Guanyin, Bodhisattva of Compassion. People pray to Guanyin to this very day to ease their sorrows, and at last she is able to do so. In that way, all of her dearest wishes came true.

Attis and the Priests
of Cybele

8

Attis and the Priests of Cybele

I questioned whether or not to include the following two stories, and some readers may wish to skip them, as they both contain removal of a person's genitals by their own hand.

For me, however, these are not portrayals of violence, but a reflection of the very real desire to be as sexless as Barbie and Ken. The ancient eunuchs are among my asexual icons, and I love to write about them.

Cybele was a goddess in ancient Phrygia (Western Anatolia in modern Turkey) who was adopted by the Greeks and Romans. My telling of "Attis and the Priests of Cybele" is a conflation of various classical sources, including Pausanias (2nd century AD) and Ovid (1st century AD).

Were you to walk the city streets of the ancient Mediterranean, you would find many temples and many gods. Hardly a day would pass without incense burning and the clash of cymbals to proclaim a festival sacred to some deity, somewhere.

Among the many worshippers, you might well encounter the priests of Cybele; the Galli, as the Romans knew them. They were very special people, counted as neither male nor female, and endowed with the gift of prophecy. Each one was a eunuch, castrated by his own hand for love of the goddess. On sacred days, they would dance through the streets to the sound of the pipe and tambourine, their jewellery jingling and their long hair flowing in the wind.

It was said that once, a Gallus took shelter in a cave in which there was a lion. Courageously, the priest played his wild music and the lion fled away!

But how did such eunuch priests come to be? The answer lies in the tale of a shepherd and the daughter of a river god.

History repeats itself, like a serpent devouring its own tail, until one can no longer tell which came first, the serpent or the egg.

The tale goes that, in ancient Phrygia, the daemon of Mount Agdistis was once androgynous, with both male and female parts. But the gods cut off the male parts and threw them away. From that spot, there grew an almond tree. And from that tree, Nana the river god's daughter one day picked an almond. She placed it in her bosom, and from that moment became pregnant.

She was the mother of Attis. Attis the beautiful. From his earliest days, he had the face of a god and the long, curling locks of a maiden. He was brought up by shepherds and by the fauns of the forest, for a river daughter is but a fickle mother. And he was tending his flocks when Cybele saw him and fell in love.

Attis was wandering beneath the pines when the goddess Cybele came by in her chariot driven by lions. Their love came quickly, as it often does among the gods. But it was not a love to be consummated in the common way. How could it be, between two such partners? Some say that Cybele was in fact the daemon Agdistis, now shorn of male parts and solely female. And since Attis was born from those discarded loins, were they not already two halves of a whole?

Be that as it may, Attis' only desire was to tend the shrine of Cybele and worship her as a priest. This was to Cybele's liking.

"If you would do so, then desire to be a boy always," she said.

"I do so desire," said Attis. "I make this vow before you - to love only you, and never to lie with anyone."

This would have been well, but Attis' foster parents had other plans. Sensing his innate nobility, they sent him to Pessinos, secretly arranging with King Calaus that Attis might wed the king's daughter.

When Attis arrived at Calaus' court, the wedding table was already laid and the priests assembled. Calaus smiled at the beautiful youth and spread wide his hands.

"Welcome, son-in-law, to your bridal feast!"

Attis felt no desire towards Calaus' daughter, shapely though she was. He wished only to be the chaste consort of Cybele. But, as a dutiful son, how could he refuse the plans his parents had made for him? Reluctantly, he went along with the ceremony. But as the wedding song was being sung, he suddenly had a vision of Cybele riding her lion-drawn chariot, her eyes flashing with jealous anger.

"No! I will not break my vow!" he cried, and rushed into the forest.

It was there that Calaus found him, weeping under the sacred pines.

"Dear boy, put away these tears." Calaus caressed Attis' wet cheek. "Don't be so hasty to despair. There are other paths to union our families can take." Calaus leaned closer. "Beautiful boy."

Attis saw the other man's eyes brighten. Bearded lips grazed his. He leapt back in shock.

"Get away from me! I desire to lie with no one. No one. Don't you understand?"

Calaus took hold of him, more roughly this time.

"I think you protest too much, my boy. If you have no desire for a woman, then surely your tastes are for men. Why deny it?"

Before Attis knew it, his shepherd's knife was in his hand.

"Get back! I am no one but Cybele's. And I will prove it."

And with these words, he cut off his own manly parts, and collapsed beneath the tree.

From deeper in the woods, a clash of cymbals and a rumble of chariot wheels drew nearer. Calaus fled for his palace in fear. The goddess Cybele dismounted and knelt by Attis' side.

"Attis! Beloved shepherd! I beg of you, do not die! You have proved your love for me again and again. How can I lose you now?" She raised her eyes to heaven. "Father Zeus, can this man not be spared?"

But the heavens were silent.

In desperation, Cybele caused Attis' departing spirit to go into the pine tree, which henceforth would be sacred to his memory forever.

"And in memory of the love of Attis, all future priests of mine shall be eunuchs, willingly and by their own hand," Cybele declared. "So shall they prove their devotion to me, although none can be as dear as he."

And that is the reason the priests of Cybele were eunuchs. And why every year, they would cut pines to mourn the death of Attis, gentle consort of the goddess.

The Goddesses and the Boar

9

The Goddesses and the Boar

This is a Hawai'ian myth about Pele, goddess of fire and volcanos, and her sister Kapo. It appears in Folktales of Hawai'i *(1933) by Mary Kawena Pukui. In one sense, it is an origin myth about the creation of the land. But it is also a tale about a woman outwitting her would-be attacker, making a joke of his lust and standing up for her right to go unviolated. There is something appealing about the idea of being able to throw your genital organs away like a quoit, displacing the act of sexual congress from your body.*

Kamapua'a was a shape-shifter. He could appear as a handsome man, but when taken over by his basest desires, he appeared as a grunting boar with bristles on his back. In that form, he was unable to control his lust and greed. He was a male chauvinist pig long before the term had been invented.

Pele was the goddess of fire. It was she who shaped the land of Hawai'i with her volcanic lava. She dwelt in the volcano Kīlauea with her sisters the Hi'iaka and their family of fire gods. These sister-goddesses were strong women, powerful in sorcery and in the hula. Woe betide the man who dared cross them!

One day, when Pele was with her sister, the goddess Kapo, they heard the sound of drumming and looked out to see a man dancing on the plains. It was Kamapua'a. When he saw the sisters looking at him, he gyrated all the harder.

"Come on, ladies! You know you want some!" he called.

"That's not a man, that's a hog," said Pele in disgust. She knew Kamapua'a's reputation all too well. He had long desired her, but she always scorned him.

"Take a hike, pig man!" she called over her shoulder.

"You'll regret that, witch!" said Kamapua'a. "I'll have you. Wait and see."

"Ignore him, sister," said Kapo. "Come on, let's go."

But Kamapua'a was not going to let them get away so easily. He grew in size to become an enormous boar and gave chase to the sisters, ploughing a valley into the landscape with his tusks as he went. The two goddesses shifted shape to avoid him, from fire to flesh and back again. They called lava from the volcano down on Kamapua'a. In his turn, he called up water from the sea to put out the flames. Steam hissed as the gods did battle, the sisters fighting off the lustful boar with all their magic.

It seemed for a while that they had defeated him. But Kamapua'a was only biding his time. Near Puna on the Big Island of Hawai'i, in a place called Lua-o-Pele, he caught up with Pele, determined to rape her.

But quick-thinking Kapo outwitted him. Unknown to Kamapua'a, her female genital organ – her kohe – could be detached from her body. She took it off now and threw it like a quoit as far as she could.

Like a dog playing fetch with its master, Kamapua'a raced after the flying kohe. He was so filled with animal lust, that he barely noticed it had no body. Neither did he notice that, before he reached the place where it fell, Kapo had taken it back and hidden it away in the volcano Kīlauea. He went on mindlessly rutting into the earth until he had formed a cave. It is there to this day: the Cave of Kapo-kohe-lele (Kapo of the Flying Kohe).

Pele laughed in triumph when she heard how her sister had tricked Kamapua'a and put an end to his plan of violence. For a goddess's body is – and always will be – her own.

The Miracle of Marjatta

10

The Miracle of Marjatta

"The Miracle of Marjatta" is taken from the final song in Elias Lönnrot's Finnish epic, The Kalevala (1835, 1849). Lönnrot travelled Finland and Karelia in the nineteenth century, collecting songs from the oral tradition, which he fashioned into an epic story, stretching from the creation of Finland to the coming of Christianity and the departure of the old gods.

Marjatta's tale is interesting because it is a version of the Christmas story, imagined in the world of Finnish paganism. As I said in Asexual Fairy Tales, *the Virgin Mary is one of my asexual icons. In this version, Marjatta becomes pregnant by eating a berry. It reminds me of the traditional "Cherry Tree Carol" in which Joseph tells Mary to ask the father of her child to get her a cherry from the tree, at which the tree bends down to the earth before her.*

The days of the mighty shaman Väinämöinen were drawing to an end in Karelia when Marjatta was born. And yet, she had no notion that it would be she who caused the days of song-magic to end and a new day to dawn.

She was always a modest girl. Folk used to say of her that she would not go milking because the cow had been with a bull, and would not ride in a sledge drawn by a mare that had been with a stallion. But perhaps this was just hearsay. Folk in the village just felt Marjatta was different.

In truth, she had hopes and fears like any other girl. She longed to be loved, but the village boys all kept their distance. Did they believe her too good? Too cold? Marjatta did not know.

She spent her days herding sheep, up hill and down dale, beneath the branches of the alders and between the cowberry bushes. As she walked, the tin trinkets at her breast – signs of her single status – made music to harmonise with the call of the cuckoo.

"Tell me, cuckoo," said Marjatta, "will I always be alone?"

The cuckoo made no reply. But from the heath at her feet, a cowberry called out, "Eat me! Pick me! Choose me! A hundred maidens have passed me by, a thousand women have looked at me, never to touch. Pick me, Marjatta!"

The cowberry was lonely, just like her. Marjatta picked and ate it. The taste went right down to her belly. Just one little berry and already her tummy was full.

Full indeed, and soon to grow fuller. As the weeks and months went by, Marjatta began to go about unbelted, with her bodice unlaced. She crept to the sauna in secret to bathe alone. Those around her soon became suspicious.

At last, the day came when Marjatta could hide no longer. Her pains came upon her; her womb was hard and taut. She was forced to beg her mother for a warm room where she could give birth.

"Get away from me, you slut!" her mother said. "Who have you been lying with? A married man, was it? Or a passing stranger? You bring shame on me!"

Marjatta tried to explain about the cowberry, but her mother didn't understand. Her father was harsher still.

"Get off and give birth in a bear's den, where you belong!"

Marjatta begged one of the farm hirelings, a young girl named Piltti, to help her.

"Go over to Herod's cabin, and ask if I may use their sauna."

Piltti loved Marjatta, who was always kind to her. She picked up her skirts and ran like smoke on the wind, crunching over pine cones and skidding over gravel until she reached Herod's cabin. It was hard to miss; it was the biggest in the village. Herod was the village headman. The steam constantly rising from his sauna proclaimed his wealth and power to the entire neighbourhood.

Herod was drinking at the head of the table when Piltti came in. He drained his cup to the dregs and banged it down on the table with a scowl.

"What do you want here, girl?" he said.

"Please." Piltti panted hard. "My mistress is in labour and begs the use of your sauna."

Herod raised a black eyebrow and turned to the mistress of the house who sat beside him, clad in furs and amber jewellery. The lady gave a disdainful sniff.

"Our baths are not free for all and sundry. And especially not for a scarlet woman like your mistress. Tell her to take a sauna in the stable on Burnt Hill."

At that, all the assembled guests laughed.

Piltti ran back to Marjatta twice as fast. Her mistress was bent double, breathing hard against the birth pangs.

"No luck, mistress. We'll have to seek shelter on Burnt Hill."

Together they went, the one leaning heavily upon the other. When they reached the stable, they found a horse and a foal within. Marjatta sank into the straw with a sigh.

"Help me, good beasts," she pleaded. "Breathe out some steam to give me relief from my pains."

The horse and foal were only too happy to oblige, knowing how kind Marjatta was to animals. They breathed out their sweet breath, filling the stable with steam until it was as good as a sauna. There Marjatta gave birth to her baby, a little son. She held him in her arms, sang over him and fed him until both fell asleep.

When she awoke, Marjatta knew something was wrong. She looked into the pile of straw beside her. Her baby was gone.

Where could she go to seek him? Marjatta searched on the hills and among the pines, through patches of heather and under tree roots. But her baby was not to be found.

So Marjatta took to the sky. She wandered the heavens until she met a star.

"Oh, star, beautiful in creation," she said. "Have you seen my baby, the little golden apple of my eye?"

The star replied, "If I knew, I would not tell. For it is he who created me to glitter in the darkness."

So Marjatta wandered further until she met the moon.

"Oh moon, beautiful in creation, have you seen my baby, the little golden apple of my eye?"

"If I knew," said the moon, "I would not tell. For it is he who created me to keep watch over the night."

So Marjatta wandered further until she found the sun.

"Oh sun, beautiful in creation, have you seen my baby, the little golden apple of my eye?"

The sun answered wisely.

"Yes, I know of your baby. For it is he who created me to shine like gold and silver. But ill luck for him! He is in the swamp, where bastard children are left to die, up to his armpits in mire."

Marjatta flew to save her son from the miry swamp. She pulled him from the mud and held him in her arms again. A timely rescue!

But when it came to naming her son, that was another matter. She called him Little Flower and Golden Apple, for he was the delight of her eyes. But the villagers called him Fly-by-Night and Ill-Begotten because his mother was unwed. The elder of the village would not baptise him without an enquiry into his parentage.

"And who is more fit to judge this matter than Väinämöinen, the eternal wise man, who was born old and named all of creation with his song?"

That was the decision of the elder, and the villagers agreed. They must send for Väinämöinen.

Väinämöinen came, old of face and strong of body, with his beard down to his knees and his *kantale* – his Finnish harp – on his back. Väinämöinen came, and pronounced his judgement.

"This boy was born of a berry and raised from a swamp. Let him be buried in the earth beside the cowberry bush, or taken to the swamp and hit on the head with a stick!"

The elder was about to concur, as none had ever questioned Väinämöinen's judgement since the hills were first raised. But to everyone's shock, the infant himself spoke.

"Old man, you have misjudged me! For you yourself did wicked deeds in your youth worthy of a beating in the swamp, and no one questioned you. But you condemn me, who even the stars in the heavens acknowledge as Lord."

At this, the people of Karelia knew that the time of Väinämöinen was ended, for one greater than he had come. Reluctantly, Väinämöinen baptised the child and named him King of Karelia, Guardian of All Power.

Then Väinämöinen sang a last song, calling for his magical boat to come to him. When it came, he stepped aboard and bid the people farewell.

"I leave you now," he said, "but one day, I will return to you. When your need is greatest, when you acknowledge your need of Väinämöinen, then I will come again. Until such a time, I leave you my *kantele*. I leave you my music and my songs. They will be your songs, and the songs of your children's children."

So Väinämöinen left Karelia, singing. And Marjatta's child, the one born from a berry, watched him go.

Clorinda the Knight

11

Clorinda the Knight

I first came across the tale of Clorinda in an academic book, The Manly
Masquerade *(2003), by Valeria Finucci. It comes from Torquato Tasso's*
Gerusalemme liberata *(1581), an Italian romance about the Crusades,
which owes a lot of its style to Homer's* Iliad.

*It was believed in former times that the mother could unwittingly influence
the appearance of her unborn child by what she looked at during pregnancy.
What she saw could be spontaneously replicated by her womb. This could
have been an attempt to explain abnormalities of birth. The shock of a white
child born to black parents – as in this story – could be a misunderstanding
of albinism. But symbolically, it opens up all sorts of possibilities of asexual
parenthood.*

*Clorinda herself defies any attempt at a binary definition. She's a black
woman who is white, a Muslim who was born Christian, a lady who is
a knight.*

*Tasso didn't give Clorinda's mother a name, so I have used Persinna, the
name given to the queen in one of his possible sources, the Greek romance*
Aethiopica *(3rd or 4th century AD) by Heliodorus of Emesa.*

Many have heard tell of the Saracen knight, Clorinda, who
bravely defended Jerusalem against the Latin Crusaders. The
Crusader Tancred was said to have fallen in love with her on
the battlefield, to have killed her by mistake when she was in disguise,
and to have held her in his arms as she died.

Until her dying day, she believed herself a Saracen born and bred.
But before her last mission, the truth was revealed to her by the only
father she had ever known, the Egyptian eunuch, Arsete. Thus she was

revealed to be a child of three fathers, neither male nor female, neither black nor white, neither Christian nor Muslim, but a union of all these contradictions and therefore whole in herself.

This is the tale Arsete told:

In Ethiopia, there lived a king named Senapo and his beautiful queen, Persinna. This Senapo was a jealous man, fiercely protective of his queen. He feared lest another man should charm and win Persinna. So he caused his queen to be locked in a round tower, constantly guarded by the eunuch, Arsete. Though she could not go outside, the world was brought to her in the form of paintings from different lands. In this way, Persinna could at least look upon human faces, though they spoke to her not.

One of these paintings came from Anatolia, and depicted Saint George – that country's famous son – delivering the virgin Sabra from the clutches of the dragon. This was Persinna's favourite picture and she looked at it often. Perhaps she wished a Saint George would arrive for her and free her from her husband's jealous grasp.

In time, the queen fell pregnant. King Senapo eagerly anticipated an heir. But when the hour of confinement arrived, the child that was born resembled neither the king nor the queen. Instead of having the features of an Ethiopian princess, the baby girl had the pale skin and straight hair of an Anatolian.

"How can this be?" the queen gasped. She stared at the baby in disbelief.

"Majesty, it is because you have gazed so long upon the icon of Saint George," said Arsete, "for it is well known that an unborn child is shaped by its mother's imagination. Anything she looks upon can influence the child's appearance. Ah, me! You may as well say Saint George is this little girl's father."

"But what shall I do now?" Persinna struck the wall with her hand. "My husband will never believe this is his child, yet I swear I have been faithful. How could I be otherwise?" she muttered. "Whatever I may wish in my heart."

"There is only one thing we can do," Arsete said. "We must swap the child for the child of a serving woman, before the king can find out."

"Yes," said Persinna. "And then you must take my daughter away, far away from here. She must be free. She must not be imprisoned as I have been."

So, the faithful Arsete placed the baby girl in a wooden chest and covered it with leaves to hide her from prying eyes. He fled into a wild place, fearing the open highways. But soon he heard a growl and saw something moving among the trees. A tigress, her fur as shadow and flame, came prowling into the clearing. In fear, Arsete climbed a tree, leaving the babe in the box exposed. He cursed himself; had he rescued the child from the king's wrath only to have her eaten by a tiger?

The tigress approached the chest. She sniffed at the baby. Then she lay down, exposing her breasts so the child could feed. She suckled the baby as if it was her own cub, and returned to do so every day until the child could be weaned.

Arsete named the little girl Clorinda. As he was a Muslim from Egypt, he decided to return to that land with the child, and bring her up in his own faith, rather than the Coptic Orthodox faith of her parents.

The way to Egypt was long and fraught with dangers. Arsete and Clorinda suffered many adventures on the way. At one point, they were chased by thieves. The only way of escape was for Arsete to plunge into a roaring river, holding Clorinda aloft. He was sure they would drown, but to his surprise, the waters calmed as he entered them and he reached the further shore in safety.

That night, he dreamt of a knight with sword in hand and the features of an Anatolian.

"I am Saint George," said the knight. "It was I who made the tigress tame and the river mild. I did it to save Clorinda, who was born in my image. Together, you and I are her two fathers. I am an Anatolian Christian man and you are an Egyptian Muslim eunuch. Our daughter will be unique among the nations: neither male nor female, neither black nor white, neither Christian nor Muslim, but a union of all these contradictions and therefore whole in herself. Her fame will never die."

Clorinda grew up beautiful and strong. Though she was a second Sabra in looks, she took after Saint George in temperament. She despised indoor chambers, soft furnishings, the gossip and giggling of other women. She would rather be out in the field, taming and riding the famous Arabian steeds. She was swifter than Achilles. She wrestled in the sand, hunted boar, bear and lion. She loved to go into the forest, seeking out the secret haunts of satyrs, fauns and fairies, and joining in their wild revels.

In feats of arms, only Argantes was her equal. There was no tournament in which she would not tilt. Her badge was that of a tigress, emblazoned orange and black upon her helm. When war came to Jerusalem, she was first among the ranks of Aladine's army.

So it was that Tancred saw her in the battlefield and engaged her in single combat. So it was that he fell in love with her, though she was his enemy, and refused to fight her any more. So it was that she felt the only stirring of romance she had ever known, though she disguised it as hatred.

And so it was that she finally met her tragic end at the hands of her beloved. For, after hearing the tale of her birth and bidding farewell to her father Arsete, she sallied out to break the Crusaders' siege towers, dressed not in her accustomed armour but in a disguise of black.

So it was that Tancred killed her, knowing not who she was until it was too late. It is said by storytellers that she saw her father Saint George in her dying moments. May it be that she saw King Senapo and Queen Persinna too, and gained their blessing. For she was a child of many parents, unique among the nations, whose fame will never be forgotten.

The Rose of the Alhambra

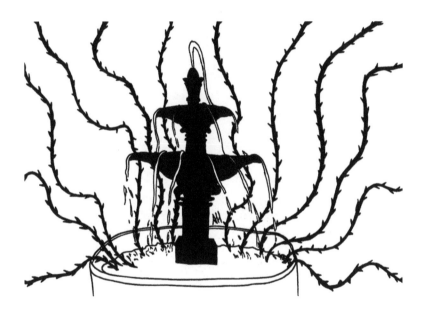

12

The Rose of the Alhambra

This is a type of Rapunzel story that is also a local legend about the Alhambra Palace in Granada, Spain. It was retold by Washington Irving in his Tales of the Alhambra *(1832). Its story-within-a-story structure reminds me of "The Glass Coffin" and "The Half-Marble Prince" (retold in* Asexual Fairy Tales*).*

I mentioned in Asexual Fairy Tales *how much I love women-in-tower stories. This one was a special treat for me when I discovered it, because it features the castrato singer Farinelli as a character. Farinelli (Carlo Broschi 1705-1782) is a huge asexual icon for me. He was the most famous castrato opera singer of his day, and became a kind of music therapist to King Philip V of Spain. The relationship between the two is portrayed in Claire van Kampen's play* Farinelli and the King *(2015), which I was lucky enough to see at the Sam Wanamaker Playhouse, London, with renowned counter-tenor Iestyn Davies as the singing voice of Farinelli.*

I n the days of Philip V, the first Bourbon king of Spain, there was a page in the service of Queen Elisabeth named Ruyz de Alarcon. He was but eighteen years of age, comely and energetic, a great favourite with the ladies at court.

The king took it into his head to visit the Alhambra Palace in Granada, once the fortress of the Moorish sultans. The old palace, which had become a haunt of owls and spiders in latter years, was repaired and decorated in a manner fit for a king. Soon, drums and trumpets resounded from the battlements once more, while silks rustled beside the tinkling fountains of the inner courtyards.

One day, Ruyz de Alarcon was walking in the gardens of the

Generalife. He had with him a favourite gyrfalcon of the queen, and was hunting with it. The hawk alighted on the battlements of a remote and lonely tower in the outer wall of the Alhambra, built on the edge of a ravine that separated the fortress from the Generalife gardens. However much Ruyz called, the falcon would not come back.

Ruyz recognised the tower. It was called the Tower of Las Infantas, or the Tower of the Princesses. Legend had it that, during the time of the Moors, three beautiful princesses had been imprisoned here by their father.

Ruyz went into the ravine and walked around, but could find no way into the tower. He decided to approach it from inside the Alhambra. He made his way back into the palace, through hall after hall, court after court, under ceilings of stars and arabesques of calligraphy, until he came to the courtyard that led to the Tower of Las Infantas.

A small garden enclosed by trellis-work overhung with myrtles stood before the tower. To reach the door, Ruyz must pass through thickets of roses, sharp with thorns. When he reached the tower, he found the door locked. Peering in through a crevice, he saw a gilt cage containing a singing bird, a tortoiseshell cat upon a chair, and a guitar decorated with ribbons leaning against a fountain.

Could it be that the old tower was still the haunt of enchanted maidens? Ruyz knocked at the door and was delighted when it was answered by a gorgeous young woman, not much younger than himself.

"My falcon has strayed into your apartments," he told the girl. "May I come in and retrieve it?"

"Oh no, that is impossible," said the girl. "My aunt has forbidden me to open the door to strangers."

Ruyz began to panic.

"To speak the truth, it is not my hawk. It belongs to the queen, and I will lose my place at court if I do not return it."

At this, the maiden relented and opened the door. Her name was Jacinta, and she was the orphan of an officer who had fallen in the wars. But to the locals, she was known as the Rose of the Alhambra. Tales of the imprisoned maiden in the tower were the stuff of local legend. It was said her aunt kept her in such strict seclusion she had never seen a man.

"Like a rose secretly blooming among the briars," people said.

Whether or not these legends were true, the two young people were very much taken with each other. It was not long before Ruyz begged the honour of kissing Jacinta's hand. Jacinta gave Ruyz the rose that decorated her hair.

"But you must go now," she said. "My aunt will soon return from Mass."

"May I see you again?" Ruyz begged.

Jacinta smiled. "Perhaps."

So began Ruyz's secret visits to Jacinta in the Tower of Las Infantas. And when the lovers could not meet, Jacinta sang songs from the window of her tower, to the accompaniment of the guitar, that Ruyz might hear her. She was an accomplished musician, and all who heard the song were moved by its mournful beauty.

All too soon, the time came for the court to return to Madrid. Imagine the horror of the aunt when she saw an Arabian steed pawing the ground by the wicket gate, and discovered among the roses a handsome youth kneeling at her niece's feet to say farewell.

"You foolish girl! Did I not warn you against the wiles of men? How could this even have happened?" she cried.

Through her sobs and tears, Jacinta told her aunt how she had met Ruyz de Alarcon when he came looking for the queen's falcon.

"And now he is gone, and I will never see him again!" Jacinta wailed.

"You'll get over him soon enough, I dare say," the aunt muttered.

But sad to tell, Jacinta did not. Having been kept in isolation for so long, she was bound to fall hard in love with the first man she met. And while Ruyz had new scenes, duties and friends to distract him, Jacinta had no one but a crusty old aunt. You may think her foolish, and maybe she was, but such were the facts.

As autumn turned to winter and winter to spring, Jacinta sat at her window, half-heartedly strumming her guitar and thinking of Ruyz. Day by day, she grew paler, her eyes red with weeping, until her aunt knew not what to do with her.

One midsummer night, Jacinta could not sleep. She sat by an alabaster fountain in the courtyard and wept bitter tears. One by one, her tears dropped into the bowl of the fountain, until the water started to bubble, to boil, to foam, to froth. Out of the bubbles rose a female figure, dressed in the garments of a Moorish princess from three hundred years ago.

"Who are you?" said Jacinta. "And how do you come to appear in this fountain?"

"My name is Zorahayda," the other replied. "I was confined to this tower in life, and now I am imprisoned here in death. I have waited three centuries for the one who will set me free."

"I?" Jacinta couldn't be more surprised. "But how can I do that? I too am a prisoner in the Tower of Las Infantas."

"That may be the very reason you can set me free," Zorahayda said. "Listen, and I will tell you my story."

I was one of three sisters, born at one birth to the wife of Muhammad the Left-Handed, fourteenth Nasrid Sultan of Granada. My eldest sister was named Zayda, the next Zorzyda, and I was the youngest.

It happened at our birth that our father consulted astrologers, who told him that great danger would surround us when we came to marriageable age. When we reached that time, he must gather us under his wings and trust no other eye to watch us.

Before that time, he considered us safe. So he sent us to a castle by the sea, under the care of our mother's former handmaid, the discreet Kadiga. It happened that while we were there, a galley came ashore bringing Christian prisoners from the wars. My sisters and I looked down, and saw three cavaliers being led into captivity. They seemed so exotic to us, so noble and sad. Each of us secretly took a cavalier to her heart and we dreamed of them often. But my dreams differed from those of my sisters, as a nightingale differs from a falcon. I knew this when they spoke to me, though I said nothing of it.

Soon the time came when we reached marriageable age. Obeying the dictates of the astrologers, our father caused the Tower of Las Infantas to be built as our new home, and he himself came to escort us back to Granada.

In order that we may not be seen, our father the sultan caused all doors and windows to be closed on our approach. A troop of black-clad horsemen rode ahead to give warning, while we rode beside our father, veiled and richly arrayed. Our white palfreys had velvet caparisons, the bits and stirrups were of gold and the bridles adorned with jewels. Silver bells on the harness tinkled as we rode, warning travellers to keep their distance, on pain of death.

As we drew near to Granada, we were passed on the road by a convoy of prisoners. Both guards and captives threw themselves face down on the ground, but three of the prisoners either refused or did not understand the order. They were the same three cavaliers my sisters and I had seen by the sea!

Imagine our joy and delight! My father, of course, was incensed and would have struck the men down, had the captain of the guard not pleaded their nobility. Instead, they were sent to the Vermilion Towers for hard labour. But as they prepared to leave, the wind blew aside our veils. The cavaliers' eyes widened at the sight of our naked faces. From that moment, they were as lost to us as we were to them.

We soon arrived in our new home: the Tower of Las Infantas. You, maiden, may have grown accustomed to its beauty, but when first I looked on them, I could have sworn the walls were made of lace. This fountain in which I am now imprisoned was surrounded by shrubs and flowers. Birds of every colour flew among the high ceilings, contained by gold and silver nets.

As soon as we were settled, my sister Zayda - always the boldest of we three - lost no time in persuading the discreet Kadiga to make an arrangement with the captain of the Vermilion Towers. The three cavaliers were sent to work in the ravine beneath our window, and at the noon of the day when the prisoners rested from their labours, they sang to us and played their guitars.

My sisters persuaded me to return a song on my silver lute, a marvellous instrument that never failed to charm its hearers.

"Play this song, sister: *The rose is hidden among the leaves, but she delights in the nightingale's song.*"

It was a secret message. The cavaliers were quick to understand Zayda's meaning, and returned a coded song of their own: *The rose's thorn has pierced the nightingale's breast..*

One song answered another, as days became weeks and weeks became months.

Then came the fateful news. The cavaliers' families had ransomed them; they were to return to Cordova. My sisters and I wept for a day and a night. But then a second message came. If we were willing to change our faith to theirs so we could be legally married, we could leave with them under cover of darkness.

"I see no problem with that," said the headstrong Zayda. "Our mother was a captive who changed her religion from Christian to Muslim. Why should we not change in the other direction?"

"I would do anything for love," said the romantic Zorayda. "Wouldn't you, Zorahayda?"

"I...suppose so," I said, but I was not too sure. I adored my cavalier. He was so noble in his deeds, so kind in his words. But to be his wife? To leave behind my home, my family, even my faith – for what? All this talk of thorns piercing breasts sent pangs through me. Could I leave the protective armour of my tower? Could I stand before a foreign priest and make vows I did not want to keep?

I loved my sisters, so I agreed to go with them. We followed the discreet Kadiga through secret underground passageways to a sally port in the fortress. There we found a rope ladder, and our three cavaliers standing in their stirrups, waiting for us to descend.

Zayda climbed down, and then Zorayda. Each in turn was lifted by their cavalier to ride pillion behind them. But when it came to my turn, my heart misgave me. I felt as though I were torn in two, unable to make the impossible decision. I unhooked the rope ladder and threw it down.

"I cannot go with you," I said. "Godspeed, my sisters. May your lives be happy."

And I watched my sisters and my cavalier ride away without me.

That is the last I saw of them, or of the outside world. I spent the rest of my days in my tower. I never married. I kept my lost cavalier in my heart until my last breath. And when I died, this is where I was buried. Yet I cannot rest in peace. My spirit still longs for my cavalier to return. I wish now that I had gone with him. My choice need not have been all or nothing. We might have made a different sort of marriage, a union of hearts.

"What was the cavalier's name?" said Jacinta.

Zorahayda named him. Jacinta gave a little shriek.

"But he was my ancestor. Way back, on my mother's side. The family always said he had a long-lost love somewhere, but I didn't know it was you. They say he spoke of you even on his deathbed – the rose in the tower. I think he always regretted you."

Zorahayda's tears flowed into the fountain. "Now I know you are my deliverer! Living in this tower, pining for love as I once did, you are a sister to me. And the blood of my cavalier flows in your veins. In you, the fragmented parts of me are knit together. You can make me whole again.

"This is what you must do. Take water from this fountain in your hands and pour it over my head. As you do, say the words: *Be whole, be free, be who you are meant to be.* God will reward you for this, my sister, with a gift to free you from your troubles."

Jacinta did as she was asked. She scooped water from the fountain into her cupped hands and poured it over Zorahayda's head, speaking the healing words. With a blissful sigh, Zorahayda dissolved into a fine mist and vanished. In her place, resting against the bowl of the fountain, was a silver lute. It was the finest instrument Jacinta had ever seen. Its body was engraved with foliage and fruit; its head was topped with a silver phoenix. Jacinta plucked one of the strings; a note as sweet as honey plucked the very strings of her heart.

"Thank you, Zorahayda," she whispered.

In the morning, Jacinta told her aunt all that had happened. She showed her the lute, and played it. The music it made rivalled the harps of paradise. Every note was an enchantment. The flinty and sceptical aunt was enraptured by the music and by the tale of Zorahayda.

"My child, this is marvellous," she said. "The romance of the old tower is alive once more. Ah! I can almost imagine myself one of the princesses of old, pining for her lost cavalier."

Jacinta, who had pined for her page all this time with no sympathy from her aunt, raised an eyebrow at this. But the more she played, the more enchanted the old woman was. And not only she. Every traveller who passed by the tower stopped, spellbound by the music. Even the birds of the air stopped their song and gathered on branches by the window to listen.

Soon, people from around Granada sent messages to the tower, begging Jacinta to come and play for them. Instead of refusing them, the aunt was as keen as anyone for Jacinta to perform.

"This music cannot be contained in a tower," she said. "Let us go forth and take your music to the people."

Jacinta travelled from town to town, and from city to city, playing the silver lute. Before long, the wealthy and powerful were vying to be her patrons. She became the guest of every great house and fashionable salon in Andalusia. From Cordova to Malaga to Seville, wherever she went she was greeted with praise.

Meanwhile, at the court of King Philip V, a very different mood prevailed. History relates that the king suffered from melancholia and all kinds of sick fancies. He would take to his bed for days on end, scratch and bite himself, and even believe himself changed into a frog. The most effective cure for his troubles was music, and the queen had gone to great lengths to employ the singer Farinelli as a kind of musical physician. The celebrated castrato would be summoned to sing arias at all hours of day or night to soothe the king's sick spirits.

But now a new torment had come upon the king. He believed himself to be dead. He insisted on having funeral ceremonies performed over him, then berated the courtiers for failing to bury him. Even the music of Farinelli could not soothe him; the queen and ministers were at their wits' end for what to do.

Then someone heard tell of Jacinta and the silver lute. She was brought with all speed to Madrid and taken to a darkened chamber hung with black, deep in the royal palace. There, in the midst of burning candles was a funeral bier, upon which lay the King of Spain, his arms folded across his breast.

Jacinta began to play. Plucking the strings of the silver lute, she sang of the Alhambra's ancient glories in the time of Muhammad the Left-Handed. She sang of the three princesses in the Tower of Las Infantas, of the yearning of the nightingale for the rose. She sang the song of Zorahayda, imprisoned in the fountain because she was forced to choose between love and inviolability. Each of the courtiers imagined himself among the filigree latticework and tinkling fountains of the inner gardens and felt the sweet sorrow of love that can never be requited, yet can never grow stale. A tear fell on each cheek.

The king opened his eyes. He sat up. He leapt to his feet and called for his sword.

"What am I doing in this chamber of death? I am alive!" he cried.

The court was overjoyed at the recovery of the king. The queen called Jacinta to stand before her.

"We owe you a reward for this service. Ask for anything you want," she said.

"I ask but one thing of your majesty," Jacinta said. And she glanced at the waiting crowd of courtiers, where she thought she saw a familiar face. "Grant me permission to resume my courtship with your page, Ruyz de Alarcon. For he left me bereft in the Alhambra, and I would discover if we can forge a relationship to suit us both, as a wise princess once said."

"With pleasure, my dear," said the queen.

And that is where Jacinta's story ends. I leave it for you to determine if she and Ruyz were happy together.

As for the lute, which had brought the king back from the dead, it became one of the treasures of the court, while Philip lived, at least. When the king died for real, much changed at the court of Madrid. Farinelli, whom the king had honoured as a cavalier, was dismissed by his successor Charles III. He returned to his home in Bologna, taking the silver lute with him, for he had heard in its notes a song he knew, a song of love beyond bodies. There were some who said it was the power of the lute that kept Farinelli singing into old age, after many of his fellow castrati had lost their voices.

After that, the lute passed into other hands, who were ignorant of its mystic powers. They melted down its silver and transferred its strings to a Cremona violin. Strange to tell, their power to enchant remained undiminished in their new setting. That violin went on to bewitch the world – as the fiddle of Paganini!

The Snow Maiden

13

The Snow Maiden

The story of "Snegurochka" – The Snow Maiden – appears in many forms. There is a version in Old Peter's Russian Tales *(1916) by Arthur Ransome, called "Little Daughter of the Snow", and one called "Snowflake" in Andrew Lang's* Pink Fairy Book. *All tell of a maiden of snow coming to life in the human world only to melt away, but the reason for her melting differs from tale to tale.*

My version is mainly based upon the opera The Snow Maiden *by Nikolay Rimsky-Korsakov, which premiered in 1882 at the Mariinsky Theatre, St Petersburg. The opera itself was based on a 1873 play by Alexander Ostrovsky. It is this version that introduces the idea that Snegurochka will melt if she falls in love. The portrayal of Snegurochka as somehow less than human because she can't love resonates with contemporary experience of aphobia and ace erasure.*

This version gives Snegurochka two contrasting suitors, Lel and Mizguir. Is what Snegurochka feels for Lel aromantic attraction? Does Mizguir represent sexual love? I'll leave it for you to decide.

The play also inspired a 1878 ballet by Marius Petipa, which I watched online during the course of my research. I can highly recommend it.

Many thousands of years ago, when Nature Spirits still walked the earth, Father Frost the Winter King fell in love with the Beautiful Spring, and she with him.

It should have been against both their natures, but such is the way of love. It often transcends what is considered natural. But Nature is apt to resist. Spring bore Father Frost a daughter, whom they named Snegurochka, the Snow Maiden. But from the time of her birth, Winter reigned over the Land of the Bevendeyans. The seasons never turned. And Snegurochka was kept close by her father, in a cabin deep in the woods, guarded by the spirits of the forest.

However, her father could not be with her all the time. He had blizzards to call up and icicles to form. And the forest guardians were not always as watchful as they might have been. So it was that Snegurochka often wandered from her cabin and hid among the snow-clad trees to watch the humans.

One of these humans was the shepherd boy Lel, who often wandered the forest paths playing his flute to the birds and beasts. It was a wonder to see the timid creatures creep forth from their hiding places at the sound of Lel's music and sit with twitching ears, as if enjoying every note.

But Lel was not always alone with the forest creatures. Snegurochka noticed he was a handsome youth, with high cheekbones and a lithe figure. The village girls noticed it, too. They would chase after Lel and dance around him, begging him for a kiss. Or sometimes they would cover his eyes and hide among the trees, calling out to him in shrill voices, daring him to seek them.

Snegurochka watched all this in wonder. What was the meaning of these games? What would it be like to be a human and have companions to chase about the woods? More and more often, she crept close to the village to watch its comings and goings, its work and its festivals. More and more, she felt lonely in her cabin, with none but wood sprites for company.

The next time her father visited, she made a request.

"Father, I beg to be born as a human and live my life as one of them."

Father Frost was shocked by this request, and sent for Snegurochka's mother, the Beautiful Spring.

"What is this, my snowflake?" Spring said. "You wish to live among humans?"

"Yes!" Snegurochka clapped her hands. "I wish to be a human and dance with the beautiful Lel. His music makes my heart sing, and his face delights me."

"My daughter," Father Frost scowled, "I must tell you now that it is impossible for you to feel love. If you ever did, you would melt away."

But Snegurochka insisted that she wished to be human.

"Very well," said the Beautiful Spring. "It shall be so. But if you are ever in trouble, call on me and I will come to your aid."

In the village of the Bevendeyans lived an old couple named Bobyl and Boblinka. For many years they lived in hope of having a child, but now so many years had passed that they had resigned themselves to childlessness.

One day when the sun was shining, Bobyl and Boblinka stood at the door of their hut, watching the boys and girls make snowmen. Their happy laughter brought a tear to Boblinka's eye.

"If only we could have had a child."

Bobyl touched her arm.

"Let's make a snow child. Come on, we're not too old for fun and games! It will warm our old bones and gladden our hearts."

So the old people ran out into the snow, much to the children's amusement, and busied themselves making a child of snow.

"Let's make it a girl," said Boblinka. "I always wanted a daughter."

When the snow girl was made, the couple stood back to admire their handiwork.

Just then, the snow child began to shiver and shake. It shone with a silver light that made the old couple screw up their eyes. When they could look again, instead of a snow girl, there stood Snegurochka. She had been born a human, just as she wished.

Snegurochka was the daughter Bobyl and Boblinka had always dreamed of. She helped her new parents with their chores and was often singing and merry. But she would never sit too close to the stove, preferring a seat by the door where the icy wind whistled through the cracks. She would often go into the forest, which worried Bobyl very much at first. But every time she came back, she was always accompanied by a little red fox. Bobyl began to think the fox was taking care of her, which of course it was, for it was one of the forest spirits in disguise.

But Snegurochka's greatest delight was to sit in the window at the evening hour, when the music of rams' horns announced that the shepherds were coming home from the hills. Then she could run to the door of the hut, in order to see Lel as he passed.

"Play me a song, Lel. Please."

"What will you give me for my song?" asked Lel one night. "Will you give me a kiss?"

Snegurochka screwed up her face. She had seen young couples planting kisses on lips and cheeks. It seemed a pointless action.

"Oh no, your song is worth much more than that! I will give you this beautiful winter flower. See how delicate its petals are, yet it thrives among the snowdrifts. It is a true treasure. Here! I will put it in your buttonhole."

Now it was Lel's turn to make a face.

"What do I want with a flower? It will only fade away." He turned towards the other village girls who crept towards him, giggling. "Which one of you can catch me and earn a kiss?"

As Lel and the girls ran off together, Snegurochka's heart ached.

"Why does Lel like those other girls more than me? Oh Mother, being human hurts!"

At the same time, another maiden in the village was preparing for her wedding. Koupava was betrothed to the merchant Mizguir. Both she and her parents approved the match, for he had paid a price in gold coins almost as handsome as he was. With his curling beard and broad chest, he was more than a youth, yet young enough to be vigorous. In Koupava's mind, the wedding couldn't come soon enough.

Koupava had made friends with Snegurochka since she had come to the village. So it was only natural that at the betrothal ceremony she called Snegurochka into the circle of maidens to dance their last dance with Koupava before she became a bride.

But when Mizguir laid eyes on Snegurochka, he became as one bewitched.

"Who is that?" he gasped. I have never seen such beauty in my life. Tell me the maiden's name."

"That is Snegurochka," the villagers said. "Adopted daughter of Bobyl and Boblinka."

"Snegurochka," Mizguir breathed.

And from that moment, he paid no more attention to Koupava than he would a wooden doll.

Koupava was distraught. She pleaded and enticed Mizguir, scolded and cursed him, but it made no difference. Snegurochka, for her part, was baffled. Why did Mizguir keep following her instead of Koupava? Didn't those two belong together, like Bobyl and Boblinka, like Father Frost and Beautiful Spring? She only wanted Lel, not this man as broad and hairy as a bear!

"I've changed my mind," Mizguir announced. "I will no longer wed Koupava. I love the maiden Snegurochka.

At this Koupava became hysterical.

"I thought you were my friend!" she screamed at Snegurochka. "And you, Mizguir, you have insulted both me and my family!"

As she collapsed, sobbing, to the ground, Lel ran to support her.

The betrothal disaster caused such a stir in the village that the elders decided the only thing to be done was to take the case to the Tsar himself. In those days, the Tsar's court travelled about the land, so the Little Father could judge his subjects fairly. In due time the Tsar arrived in that place, setting up his pavilion in the village square. Koupava's parents stood before the golden throne and begged the Tsar to hear their case.

"Little Father, Mizguir must be made to marry our daughter," they pleaded.

Most of the villagers agreed. But Mizguir insisted he only loved Snegurochka.

"And I won't marry Mizguir. The two-faced beast!" Koupava said, putting an arm around Lel.

"In that case, Mizguir must be banished," the Tsar said.

Mizguir fell on his knees.

"Little Father, please! Only see Snegurochka and you will understand."

Snegurochka was called to appear. The Tsar was intrigued. She was undoubtedly a young woman in her prime, but pale as ice and delicate as a frost flower. The hairs on the back of the Tsar's neck stood on end. Many years ago, he had heard a prophecy from the priest of the Sun God that the melting of a Snow Maiden's heart would bring an end to winter. Could this be the promised Snow Maiden?

"My child, do you love this man?" The Tsar pointed to Mizguir.

Snegurochka looked from Mizguir to Lel and back again.

"I like…" she began, then shut her mouth. She liked Lel. He was pretty and made such beautiful music. But was that what the Tsar meant by love?

"I like Lel," she said.

"You are in love with the shepherd Lel?" The Tsar's tone was serious.

"I don't know," said Snegurochka. "Do you think I am?"

There was a gasp from the assembly. Boblinka stepped forward, trembling.

"Little Father, she doesn't understand what being in love is. It's not in her nature. But she's a good girl."

"Not in her nature to be in love? And because of this frozen heart we are cursed with endless winter," the Tsar muttered. Aloud, he said, "Whoever can make Snegurochka fall in love with him before another sun rises shall be richly rewarded from my own coffers when he takes her to wife."

"Lel can do it," someone said. "Lel makes all the girls fall in love with him."

"And then Mizguir will return to our daughter," Koupava's parents muttered.

Snegurochka smiled. Now Lel would like her best of all and forget the other village girls. The Tsar had spoken. She and Lel would make music and dance together, just as she had wished.

The contest began immediately. Lel took out his flute to play, and the youths and maidens of the village danced a circle around him. Each wore a crown of flowers on their head. Snegurochka danced up to Lel and placed a flowery crown on his head while he played on. A whole crown of flowers was better than a single bloom! Now Lel would understand how much she liked him.

When the music stopped, the watching Tsar gave his command.

"Youths and maids, now is the time to choose your sweethearts. I will bless any matches made today." He looked at Lel. "You too, young shepherd. Will you now choose the fair Snegurochka? Have you won her heart?"

"Oh, choose me! Choose me, Lel!" Snegurochka stood on her tiptoes.

"Her heart is ice," Lel said. He went and put his arm around Koupava. "This is the bride I choose. A complete woman, who will warm my bed and satisfy my heart. Not a cold Snow Maiden whose only gift is flowers."

Snegurochka gave a cry of anguish. Lel had betrayed her! And Koupava too. How could they?

As she watched, Lel led Koupava to the Tsar, and kissed her in the presence of all the villagers. The Tsar stood and everyone followed him to bless the match at the shrine of the Sun God.

Snegurochka stood sobbing.

"Lel! Beautiful Lel. How could you abandon me? Am I not pretty enough? Am I boring and stupid? I can love you too, I know I can. Just give me time. Don't leave me, Lel!"

She was sobbing so hard that she didn't notice Mizguir until he whispered in her ear. "Forget the boy. I'll show you how a real man loves." He seized her hand and pressed it to his lips.

"No! Get off me!" Snegurochka snatched her hand back. "I don't want you. I want Lel."

"Lel? What can the shepherd boy give you? In my house, you'll want for nothing. I'll treat you like the princess you are."

"I don't love you," said Snegurochka.

"And you don't love Lel, either. It's just an infatuation." Mizguir ran a finger along her jawline. "Sweet, beautiful Snegurochka. You have not yet awoken to the stirrings of love. But I can thaw that chilly heart. You will fall in love with me, just wait and see."

"Stop it! Go away!" Snegurochka pushed Mizguir away and ran into the forest, the little red fox at her heels.

"Mother! Mother, I need you!" she cried.

In a twinkling, the Beautiful Spring appeared beside her daughter, and put her fragrant arms about her.

"Don't weep, little daughter. Whatever is the matter?"

"I need to love. I want to love. I'm sick of everyone saying I have a cold heart."

The Beautiful Spring looked at her seriously.

"Snegurochka, remember your father's warning. It is not in your nature to fall in love. If you do, you will melt away." She stroked her daughter's hair. "Isn't it time you came home? Leave the humans to their ways. Your father and I will always love you despite our differences, and the little red fox will always be true."

But Snegurochka only wept more.

"I want to be properly human. I want to love, so I can get married like they do and not be alone. I don't want Koupava to have what I can't have. I'm tired of being a Snow Maiden."

Spring kissed her daughter's forehead.

"My child, you are as human as they are. You don't need to fall in love for that. If you try to change your nature, you will break. Ah! But I cannot bear your tears. Your wish is granted. I give you the gift of love."

And she disappeared into the forest, taking the fox with her.

Snegurochka returned to the village. With every step she took, her heart grew warmer. Every bush, every flower seemed brighter, more fragrant than before. And was that a patch of green grass she saw? Were new leaves starting to bud where once only bare branches had been?

As she reached the edge of the forest, Mizguir came running to meet her.

"Where have you been, my love? I searched the forest all night. Oh, thank the Sun God you are safe!"

He took Snegurochka in his arms. As he did so, she felt a stirring within, a new sensation like the ripening of corn or the rising of dough.

"I'm in love!" she exclaimed. "Oh Mizguir, I'm finally in love!"

"Then let us hurry to the Tsar. No time to lose."

Mizguir took her hand and they ran through the village to the place where the Tsar had set up his pavilion. But what was this new sensation Snegurochka was feeling? Her heart was light, but her knees were weak. And was it her imagination or did the sun shine stronger than before? It hurt her head.

"Little Father!" Mizguir cried in joy. "Bless our match, for Snegurochka is in love with me and will be my bride."

"Praise to the Sun God!" The Tsar lifted his arms to pronounce the blessing. Mizguir drew Snegurochka close and they kissed, tenderly, deeply, in full view of the whole village.

Snegurochka's heart hammered. A fire was pulsing in her blood, a burning deep in her marrow. Was this ecstasy or death? It felt like both. She couldn't stand it, and yet she wanted more.

"Look!" someone cried. "Look at the Snow Maiden!"

Mizguir clutched in disbelief at the sodden dress in his arms. At his feet lay a pool of water.

"Snegurochka!" he cried. But his words were mere air.

The Snow Maiden had melted. And with her death, the first sun of spring rose strong and bright over the Land of the Bevendeyans. The first spring in fifteen years.

Children of Wax

14

Children of Wax

Though it comes from a completely different climate, "Children of Wax"
shares a theme with "The Snow Maiden". Both tales are about a character
who will melt if they try to alter or deny their true nature. But unlike
Snegurochka, Ngwabi is one among several loving siblings, who find a way
for him to remodel himself and fly away to a new life. We could imagine
the leaves and feathers that cover him as a kind of pride flag, giving him an
identity that allows him to soar.

Wax is an interesting substance. It can be made to look uncannily like
flesh, and human waxworks have been made for magical, religious and
anatomical purposes in many cultures throughout history. This includes
saints' effigies and the "anatomical Venuses" used by Enlightenment
scientists; both are kinds of Sleeping Beauties in glass coffins. Bees themselves
were once considered androgynous and parthenogenic (able to reproduce
without fertilisation) and so came to symbolise virginity and chastity.

The story comes from Zimbabwe and is told by Alexander McCall Smith
in The Girl Who Married a Lion *(2004).*

There was once a happy family of a mother, father and several
children. They lived in a village where everyone was very similar.
But this family was different. The children were made of wax.

The parents did not know why their children were waxen. They
themselves were not made of wax, but were as other people. However,
as the children were happy and healthy in other respects, the parents
did not worry too much. They loved their children dearly and were very
proud of their family.

Being made of wax, however, the children needed special care. They could not go near fire, nor could they go out in the hot sun. So the parents had a specially constructed hut built for their children, a hut with no windows. The children stayed in this hut during the day, and at night when the sun had gone down, they came out of the hut to do their chores. They tended crops and herded cattle like other village children, and they played and chatted together like other children. They just did it all in the dark.

This was well for a time, but as the children got older, they began to wonder about the outside world. They could never travel, as the paths to other villages were beset with wild beasts during the hours of darkness. And they could not spend time with other young people their age, as they were awake when other families were asleep, and vice versa.

One of the boys – Ngwabi – longed more than anything to see the outside world. He wanted to feel the sun on his face, to see the colours of trees and hear the song of birds.

"It's no use, brother," his siblings told him. "Children of wax cannot go out in the sun. Be grateful for what you have. Being wax, we cannot feel pain. And we are strong. Twice as strong as fleshly children, if our parents are to be believed."

"But soon we will not be children at all," Ngwabi said. "Soon I will be a man, and I want to live a man's life. I know we are different, but we cannot spend all our lives in this hut as if we do not exist. I want to walk in the sun."

And however much his siblings pleaded, Ngwabi would not listen. One day when the sun was at its height, Ngwabi opened the door and ran out into the light. His siblings screamed and clutched at his clothes, but it was no use. He was gone.

How bright, how beautiful it was in the sun! Birds flitted past like jewels. Flowers breathed their perfumed scent. Ngwabi saw the brightly coloured clothes of the village women as they stirred their cooking pots. Such a delicious smell! He heard the laughter of children playing, the song of young people working in the fields. Men with sweat on their backs scythed the crops. Old people sat in the shade, fanning themselves with leaves. It was more wonderful than Ngwabi could have imagined.

Alas, he had but minutes to enjoy it. In the noontime heat, he quickly began to melt. Ngwabi felt himself grow weaker and weaker, until he was nothing but a pool of wax by the door of his hut.

Inside the hut, his siblings wept and wailed. When at last the sun had set, they crept from their hut, singing funeral songs. They scraped up the molten wax that was their brother and carried it back to the hut.

There they began to work on it, moulding the wax into a new shape, the shape of a bird. They gathered fallen leaves to cover its body so no wax showed, and stuck in fallen feathers to make wings and a tail. Then they carried the waxen bird to their parents, singing and weeping all the while.

"This is Ngwabi," they told their mother and father. "He went into the sun and melted. He wanted to be free, to travel and live the life of a man. We have made him into a bird. Please can you help?"

The grieving parents kissed the bird and wept. They told their children, "Go back to your hut and keep watch."

Then they took Bird-Ngwabi and placed him on a high rock in view of their children's hut. The siblings peeped through a crack in the wall as the sky lightened and darkness turned to dawn.

When the first rays of sun fell on the rock, the feathers of Bird-Ngwabi glowed pink with fire. As the sun grew stronger, they shone gold, then bright white. Bird-Ngwabi opened his wings and took off, soaring higher and higher into the sky. Soon, he was a mere speck against the clouds.

In the hut, the siblings turned to one another and embraced. Their brother Ngwabi had found freedom.

The Little White Bird

15

The Little White Bird

JM Barrie – like Hans Andersen – is an author whose sexuality has been hotly debated over the years. Was he asexual? We will never know for sure.

The Little White Bird or Adventures in Kensington Gardens (1902) is the first of Barrie's writings to feature Peter Pan, as a sub-plot in the middle of the book. But its main plot is a stranger and more intriguing tale about a single man who wants to be a father. In particular, he wishes to be the father of a child he meets in Kensington Gardens. It is this story I have taken as a basis for my loose retelling.

Many readers will recognise some of the scenes from the 2004 film Finding Neverland, which combines the real-life story of Barrie's relationship with the Llewelyn Davies family with the fictionalised versions Barrie creates in The Little White Bird and Peter Pan.

JM Barrie's relationship with the Llewelyn Davies boys has remained a controversial one. But whatever the true facts may be, what struck me when retelling this story was the difficulty of writing about a man who wishes for a child (as opposed to a woman who wishes for a child) without it coming across as perverse. That should not be the case. Particularly when the man you are writing about is an asexual character.

There was once a man who wished for a child.

He was very fond of babies and dearly wished to become a father, but he had no desire to make babies in the usual way. Even the smiles of ladies made him uneasy.

He was an Edwardian Gentleman, the type who sat in a leather armchair at his club, reading the newspapers and drinking port. Every day, he would walk in the park with Porthos, his St Bernard dog.

Every day, he sat on the same bench, watching the birds pecking for food and the children playing. The children would come up to him, asking if they could stroke his dog. He would speak to them kindly, tell them stories and show them magic tricks. Sometimes, a very little child would call him "Father" by mistake. It warmed his heart for a moment. But then the child had to go home with its mother or nanny, and the Gentleman would remember again that he would never have children of his own.

Now the park where this Gentleman walked was a magical one. There were two sacred wells there, and ghosts walked its paths regularly. In particular, it was the haunt of fairies, who hid among the flowers by day, but by night held their revels beneath the trees. Their Queen lived in a palace of many-coloured glass that could only be seen at night, and was known to grant wishes to mortals who pleased her.

One night after the gates were shut, the Gentleman climbed the railings and crept into the park unseen. He followed the dancing lights to the Seven Spanish Chestnut Trees, and there were the fairies, dancing in a ring on a carpet of lilac blossom.

"Madam," he said, bowing low before the Fairy Queen, "I would beg a boon of you."

The Queen's glittering eyes widened.

"What an unusual mortal! Your kind cannot usually see us or speak with us after the age of five, whereas you look closer to fifty. You please me, stranger. What is your request?"

"Madam, I wish for a child of my own to love and to cherish."

All around him, the fairies laughed, a tinkling of silver bells.

"You need not come to me for that, mortal. Surely you know that all children live as birds in this enchanted park before they are born as babies. All you need do is catch one with a red ribbon around its leg, and you will have a child."

At this, the Gentleman became sad.

"I did know about the birds," he said, "and I have tried many times to catch one. But they only come to ladies. Never to me."

The Fairy Queen shrugged and turned to leave, for such is the way of fairies with mortals. But the Gentleman got to his knees and begged.

"Please. All I want is a child."

At last, the Queen said, "My fairies could make you a child, out of your shadow. But it would only ever be the shadow of a child."

"Do it," the Gentleman said, because he wanted a child so much.

So the fairies cut and snipped and stitched his shadow, until they had formed the shape of a child. It was a little boy. The Gentleman decided to call him Timothy. He thanked the fairies and took the shadow child home to his house.

For a while, the Gentleman took great care of Timothy. He bought toys for him at the toy shop. He boasted about Timothy's achievements to other parents in the park. He even bought little vests and pinafores for Timothy to wear. But alas, none of these were of any use to Timothy, because he was only the shadow of a child. Porthos the dog played with all his toys. The little clothes lay folded and useless in a drawer. Not one little vest could Timothy wear.

To make matters worse, the Gentleman and Porthos had met a little boy called David. He came to their bench in the park every day, along with his nanny. He giggled at the slightest thing, with a laugh just like that of the fairies. He ran around with his arms outstretched, as if he still remembered the time when he was a bird. His innocent chatter brought a tear to the Gentleman's eye.

It was no good, the Gentleman thought. However well behaved Timothy was, he was only the shadow of a child. He was no substitute for a real child one could cuddle, and bounce on your knee, and tuck into bed.

He went back to the Fairy Queen.

"Madam, a shadow child is not enough for me." He sighed deeply. "I wish, I wish that I could be David's father."

"David already has a father," said the Fairy Queen. "As you well know. But I will allow you to become his fairy godfather. I am convinced you must have fairy blood in your veins to be able to speak with us as you do."

A hansom cab appeared at the park gates.

"Take that cab," said the Fairy Queen, "and tell the driver to go back six years. When you get there, go to your club and watch through the window."

*

127

The Gentleman did as he was told. He paid the driver, and the cab began to drive backwards in time, until the shop on the corner sold fish instead of books and the fashions looked ever so slightly outmoded. As the Queen had instructed, he alighted, went into his club and waited.

He soon became accustomed to living in the past, and discovered that, every Thursday, a nursery governess and an artist met outside the post office. Fairy wisdom told him they must be David's parents. Interested, he kept watching until, one week, the artist failed to appear. The governess stood outside the post office, her eyes red from crying. Meanwhile, the artist hid on a street corner, watching the governess but lacking the courage to apologise for whatever he'd done.

Now was the Gentleman's chance to play a part in David's birth! He hurried into the street with a letter he had been writing, and dropped it at the feet of the artist, as if by accident. The artist saw the letter, took it to the post office and - oh, joyous reunion! - the happy couple embraced one another with tears in their eyes.

David was saved! He would no longer flit around the park as a little white bird, but be born as a real boy. The Gentleman was a real, live fairy godfather.

He began to send secret gifts to the little family in order to provide for David. He bought the artist's paintings and redeemed the mother's watch from the pawnbroker's. A doll's house and a rocking horse were delivered in secret to the nursery. The daughter of one of the club waiters was sent to the family as a nanny. The Gentleman enjoyed watching from a distance, chuckling with secret delight.

But as the past caught up to the present, the Gentleman became restive once more. A fairy godparent is not always a good thing. Fairies are apt to steal children away; and the more of a fairy godfather the Gentleman became, the greater his desire to steal David from his parents altogether. He took long rambles around the park with David and his nanny, telling him stories about the fairies. He took David shopping, delighted when the shopkeeper mistook him for David's father. And in his enthusiasm, he did something truly dreadful.

You have not forgotten the little shadow boy, Timothy? The Gentleman tried his best to forget him, for he had David in his life now. But his neighbours - and David's parents - would keep asking him how

Timothy was doing. So the Gentleman told his neighbours that Timothy was dead.

"He is no more," he said to David's father. And he gave all of Timothy's clothes to David.

He wondered if the Fairy Queen would punish him for that. But there was no need for the fairies to step in; life brings its own punishment. David began to grow up. He became interested in cricket and in tales of the hero Achilles. He tagged along after older boys who went to school. The Gentleman's heart sank. Once David went to school, he would no longer want to play in the fairy gardens or trouble himself about a Gentleman with a dog who sat on a park bench. He would be lost.

He went back to the Fairy Queen and said, "Madam, my mother told me the fairies are cruel, and she was right. You have taunted me with David. I was never his father, and now he will grow up and forget me."

"You wish for a loyal child who will stay with you and love you above all others?"

"Yes!" cried the Gentleman.

At this, all the fairies laughed. Their laughter no longer sounded like silver bells. It was heartless laughter, and the Gentleman knew they were laughing at him.

"Foolish mortal! You had that all along," said the Fairy Queen. "Go home, and tomorrow you will see."

So the Gentleman went home, and when he woke in the morning, Porthos the dog was nowhere to be found. The Gentleman searched and called his name, but all in vain. He returned to the park, thinking Porthos might be there. He was not. Eventually, the Gentleman came to his favourite bench, only to find someone sitting there. It was a portly young man with a wistful expression, who introduced himself as William Paterson. He and the Gentleman began to talk, and Paterson enjoyed the Gentleman's stories as much as any child.

The Gentleman was soon meeting with Paterson every day. Together, they lunched at the club and sat in his rooms, chatting by the fire. The Gentleman was constantly astonished by how innocent Paterson was for a man in his twenties.

"You have such touching faith in humanity, my dear boy," the

Gentleman would say. "I wish I still had your outlook. I'm nothing but an old curmudgeon.

"No, no, I won't allow that at all," Paterson insisted. "You're the best of men. A hero to put Achilles to shame."

And whatever the Gentleman said, Paterson would not hear a bad word spoken of him.

The Gentleman began to find this hero worship embarrassing. And he began to notice odd things about Paterson. He could leap the park railings in a single bound. He spread newspaper on the sofa before he would sit on it. He ate the bones of his chop as well as the meat. The Gentleman started to suspect the truth. He guessed who Paterson really was. He also saw a more uncomfortable truth. He could not bear for another person to love him as intensely as did his dog.

"We cannot go on like this," the Gentleman said at last. "I think you come from a kinder world. Are you sure you were wise in leaving it?"

Paterson said nothing.

"Why did you come like this?" the Gentleman asked.

Paterson looked at him with soulful eyes.

"I wanted to know you. I wanted to be like you," he said, and walked away.

The next day, Porthos returned, and Paterson was never seen again. Resigned, the Gentleman went back to the Fairy Queen.

"I see things clearly now," he said. "I am a lonely old man with no one to love but my dog." He glanced around at the fairies' solemn faces. "I should have been content with Timothy."

"You killed Timothy." The Fairy Queen's eyes were as ice.

"Can a shadow child be killed?" asked the Gentleman. "I'm sorry for what I did. Couldn't I have him back?"

"No," said the Fairy Queen. "And no, to both questions. Timothy lives among the fairies now. We have adopted him and given him a new name. He is a Betwixt-and-Between child, not exactly a human, nor a bird, nor a fairy. He is a boy who will never grow up and forget how to fly."

"And may I not see him?" The Gentleman looked as wistful as Paterson.

The Fairy Queen thought for a while.

"You may have his stories. As his father, I can give you that much. All your life, you may tell his stories. They will express things that you can never say. They will bring wonder and delight to children as yet unborn. For your shadow child can never die, as long as children believe in him."

"And how long will that be?" asked the Gentleman.

"Go home, mortal," said the Fairy Queen, "and write your stories." And she smiled.

The Asexual Planet

16

The Asexual Planet

The story of "The Asexual Planet" comes from Phantastes (1858) *by George MacDonald. It is one of the stories read by the main character, Anodos, in the library of the Fairy Palace. In the book, the story has no name, so I have invented one.*

George MacDonald was a Scottish clergyman and writer of fairy tales such as The Princess and the Goblin *and* At the Back of the North Wind. *He was a mentor to Lewis Carroll (the* Alice *books share many themes and motifs with* Phantastes) *and was a huge influence on CS Lewis.*

Some people dislike stories that associate asexuality with the kind of asexual reproduction found in nature, as this is not what the term asexual *means when it describes a person's identity. But I cannot help but be drawn to a tale that explores ideas of gender identity, parenthood without sex, and a world in which asexuality is the norm.*

I am a traveller beyond the sun. I pilot my craft among the stars in search of new lands, fresh experiences and novel customs. In my travels I came upon a far-off planet, a world that is not like ours, but which has remained in my heart ever since.

It is a world of great beauty, of seas and lakes and snow-capped mountains. But the waters do not reflect the forms of nature, as they do in our world. No ship sends a long, wavering reflection to the shore. No one smiles at their own face in a forest well. The sun and moon cast a glitter upon the dark waters, but that is all.

Instead, the sky reflects everything beneath it: forest and field, sea and shore. It lights up with gorgeous colours of emerald, russet, periwinkle, gold. At night, the sky appears as an egg-shaped cupola, fretted with golden fires. I have gazed upon it nights without number, losing myself in its burning glory.

The children of that world are not born as our children are. Instead, it happens thus: a maiden will go out walking alone, perhaps in the woods or along the riverbank. She goes looking for children as maidens in our world go looking for flowers. Stilling her senses, she will hear a cry from the shelter of a rock or a clump of bushes. She will search out the place until she finds a little child, nestled in the spot as if it has grown there. Joyfully, she will carry it home, calling, "Mother! I have got a baby! I have found a child!"

Her mother comes running, and soon the whole village gathers around her to share in the joyous occasion. For this will be the woman's only child and greatly treasured.

"Where did you find it? In what season? At what time of day?"

The questions fly from mouth to mouth, questions of great import. For the appearance, the personality, indeed the entire destiny of a child depends on when and where they were found, in what weather and under what stars. The morning sun will often guide a maiden to where a golden-haired boy lies in the shelter of a rock. The evenstar might rise to illuminate the pale cheek of a girl, sleeping in a nest of grass and daisies.

As they grow up, boys and girls come to lead distinct lives. For there is a peculiar difference between the men and women of that planet. The men look much as ours do, with two arms and two legs. But the women have no arms. Instead they have wings. Resplendent wings, in which they can cover themselves from head to foot. Thus, the women soar high in that reflective sky, while the men walk upon the ground.

By these wings alone, you may guess when a woman was born. Those who came in winter have swanlike wings of white, tipped with silver. They glitter like frost in the sun, and are tinged beneath with rose. Those born in spring have feathers of brilliant grass-green, enamelled at the edges and lined with white. The summer-born have wings of deep rose lined with gold. And those born in autumn have purple wings, lined with chestnut-brown. But the most beautiful woman I saw there had wings of deep carmine, with an inner down of soft grey. She had been found as the sun went down through a sea-fog, casting crimson shadows into a cave by the shore, where a bathing maiden saw her lying.

*

I have told you what I can of this distant world. To me, it seemed like paradise. But its inhabitants were keen to learn of my world, which was just as exotic to their ears. One day, a group of them gathered on a cliff-top by the sea. For a long time, they questioned me about the Earth, and I made the best answers I could. I told them that, in my world, women have arms, not wings.

"But how can you tell them from men?" someone said. "Yours must be an androgynous people."

"No, no, we are quite different," I said.

But here, I soon ran into trouble. How to describe the difference between male and female? What is important? What is not? Where do they overlap? I was forced into a territory I had rather avoid, and had to confess that children are not born on Earth as they are on the Asexual Planet.

"How, then, do they come?" The people wanted to know. "Where do you find them? In what circumstances?"

I did not want to answer their questions. I did not wish to speak of that which I had traversed the galaxies to avoid. Theirs was the world I had sought all my life, a world of pure beauty and light. I did not wish to sully it with that which, in my world, so often became degraded.

At length, I was compelled to describe the means of human reproduction. The terms I used were vague and clumsy; I was afraid lest my hosts wanted to know my thoughts and experiences on the matter. My cheeks became hot, until I resembled one born in the height of summer.

A dim notion of what I meant began to dawn in the minds of my listeners. Many folded their arms, or their wings, in front of them, standing like forbidding statues. I could see that the notion offended them. One woman spread her rosy pinions and flew away on the updrafts without a backwards glance.

But there was one woman and one man who – on hearing my words – looked each other deeply in the eyes for some time. Without a word, the woman walked away, her purple-and-white wings half-open behind her. She was found the next day some miles inland, lying dead beneath a withered tree, her wings folded upon her breast. They buried her where she lay, for their kind choose the spot where they die, finding one that resembles the place of their birth. I heard that the man suffered a similar fate.

Their elders told me that the main cause of death among their people is an indescribable and unfulfilled longing. When a maiden and a youth look too deeply into each other's eyes, this longing seizes them. Instead of drawing nearer, they wander alone into solitary places, and die of their desire.

I have since heard a legend, saying that those who die thus are reborn as babies on Earth. And if they find each other there, all shall go well with them.

I wonder, will anyone of my world, who feels as I do and lives in silent frustration, be born again in theirs?

A Wingless Wedding

17

A Wingless Wedding

Our final story is another tale of winged and wingless people, living on a distant planet.

I wrote "A Wingless Wedding" after reading about the dual life cycle of gall wasps. Winged females mate and lay eggs in oak roots. A wingless, asexual female emerges, crawls up the tree and lays eggs in the buds. These eggs need no male to fertilise them; they are parthenogenic. I was fascinated by this and wondered what it would be like if humanoid people had the same life cycle. How would culture develop if every other generation was asexual?

"A Wingless Wedding" takes us to a futuristic setting on another planet, yet draws on the traditions of ancient myth-making. It also shows that traditions can adapt to become more inclusive without losing their deep meaning and connection with our ancestors.

"A Wingless Wedding" was runner-up for the Mother's Milk Prize 2018 and was first published in Curious Fictions.

"**A**re you ready? The transporter is here."

I looked in the mirror, rearranging my floral headdress one last time. The bridal jewels glowed against the pale blue of my chest. It was the first time they had ever been passed from mother to daughter. Their weight suddenly felt immense. The weight of history. Not just my family history, but the history of the entire planet. I wasn't sure if I could do this.

They say every bride is nervous on her wedding day. I wouldn't know. My mother said she was. My grandmother, of course, had no wedding day and no husband. She nurtured my mother and her six identical sisters in cocoons woven from her own hair, as every Wingless on our planet had done before her. Wingless don't reproduce sexually. That's the task of their children, the Winged, who in turn have Wingless children. We're the only planet in our star system where this happens, and it's the same in every country. Customs and traditions vary, but one thing has stayed the same the world over. There has never been a Wingless wedding.

"But what do you want to get married for?" my mother had said. "You'll have children anyway."

"Yes, but Klip wants children, too."

My father screwed up his face in confusion.

"But they won't be his children. They'll be yours. He'll only be a sort of...caretaker."

I tried not to lose my temper.

"Dad, there's more to fatherhood than begetting. Just as there's more to love than sex. You must see that."

My parents struggled to understand. They had tolerated the Wingless Pride marches, the political lobbying, because they thought I would grow out of it. And Grandma, from whom I expected some sympathy, was scandalised.

"It's all the fault of these Mixed Schools. In my day, Winged and Wingless were educated separately. None of this off-world nonsense."

It's true. In Grandma's day, Winged and Wingless didn't even use the same transporters. It's still like that in some parts of the world. In the Western Landmass, children are taken from their parents as soon as they are weaned, and brought up by their grandparents' generation. Wingless girls are raised by their grandmothers; the smaller number of Wingless boys enter Houses of Brotherhood, where they are taught to follow a trade. Mixed Schools and Colleges are still a long way off in the West.

"Can't you and Klip just be friends?" This was my mother's next plea. "That's all you are, really. Just good friends."

My parents edged closer together, their wings humming with mutual concern.

In the wedding pictures, my mother's wings are cream and gold, my father's bright blue. Now both resemble a summer sky with fluffy clouds and rays of sunshine. That happens between Winged couples.

The longer they are together, the more passionately they unite, the more like one another they become. That will never happen to me and Klip. I will always be pale blue and he will be russet brown, just as we were born.

"Klip and I are in love. We want to marry. And as soon as the law is passed, we're going to do it."

In front of the world's press. And the media of the entire star system. I clutched the jewels at my neck, willing my hand to stop shaking. Klip and I were the first ever Wingless couple to marry. Our wedding would be at the Temple of Justice, with crowds of Wingless lining the street, and the whole world watching. It was meant to be a day of celebration for our cause. A day of celebration for me.

Eventually, my parents had come around.

"We just want you to be happy." Bright blue tears shone on Dad's cheeks. "If this is what you want..."

We had hugged, my slender body enveloped by their wings. As Winged, they would never really understand what it was like to live without their kind of desire. What it was like to love without their kind of desire. But I guess they figured that, if I could love them, I could love Klip, too. And Klip could love me.

But would the rest of the world understand? And all those off-world reporters, from planets where there were no wings to distinguish between the sexual and the asexual. Where people like me were all but invisible.

"Didn't you hear me calling?"

Klip was at the door. His own floral crown was on his head, and his sleeveless robe was dark gold. He looked utterly beautiful.

"Come on, everyone's waiting." His expression slowly changed. "Hey, what's wrong?"

"I'm scared, Klip. The reporters are going to ask all those stupid questions again. *How can it be love without sex? Isn't this making a mockery of marriage? What do you say to those who think Wingless should keep to their traditional roles?* I don't think I can face it."

Klip took both my hands in his. They were warm and steady.

"Listen to me. There's only one question that matters today. Do you want to marry me?"

I swallowed hard.

"Yes, Klip. I do."

He beamed all over his sharp-featured face.

"Good answer. So, let's go and do this. And forget everyone else. Today is about you and me."

He was right. We could do anything if we did it together. We took hands and walked out to the transport lawn, where our parents were waiting, their wings fluttering in the breeze. They were smiling with tears in their eyes. The sky was blue, with fluffy clouds and sunbeams.

Story Sources and Further Reading

Andersen, Hans Christian. *Stories for the Household*, London: George Routledge & Sons, 1889; repr. Chancellor Press, 1994.

Atsma, Aaron, J. "Phrygian Gods: Attis", *Theoi Project*, theoi.com/Phrygios/Attis..

"Attis: Phrygian Deity", "Great Mother of the Gods: Ancient Deity", *Encyclopaedia Britannica Online*, britannica.org, 20 July 1998.

Barrie, JM. *The Little White Bird or Adventures in Kensington Gardens*, London: Hodder & Stoughton, 1902; repr. Pook Press.

Barbier, Patrick. *The World of the Castrati*, London: Souvenir Press, 1996.

Beckwith, Martha Warren. *Hawaiian Mythology*, Yale University Press, 1940.

Bowler, Vivian ed. "Oak Tree Galls – The Home of the Gall Wasps' Larvae", *The Living Countryside*, London: Eaglemoss Publications and Orbis Publishing, 1981.

Bullfinch, Thomas. *The Age of Fable; or, Stories of Gods and Heroes*, Boston: Sanborn, Carter and Bazin, 1855.

Camphausen, Christina. "The Flying Yoni of the Goddess Kapo: A Polynesian Legend", *Yoniverse*, yoniversum.nl/yoni/kohelele, 2004.

Cherry, Kittredge. "Saint Wilgefortis: Holy bearded woman fascinates for centuries", *Q Spirit*, qspirit.net/saint-wilgefortis-bearded-woman/, 20 July 2019.

De Troyes, Chrétien. *Arthurian Romances*, tr. DDR Owen. London: Everyman, 1993.

Dudbridge, Glen. *The Legend of Miao-shan*, London: Ithaca Press, 1978.

Ebenstein, Joanna. *The Anatomical Venus*, London: Thames & Hudson, 2016.

Finucci, Valeria. *The Manly Masquerade: Masculinity, Paternity and Castration in the Italian Renaissance*, Durham & London: Duke University Press, 2003.

Grimm, J & W. *Household Stories*, London: George Routledge & Sons, 1853; repr. Chancellor Press, 1994.

Heiner, Heidi Anne ed. *Rapunzel and other Maiden in the Tower Tales from Around the World*, SurLaLune Press, 2010.

Hopkinson, Elizabeth. *My True Love Sent to Me*, Vancouver: Virtual Tales, 2009.

Irving, Washington. *The Works of Washington Irving, Vol. XV: The Alhambra*, New York: George P Putnam, 1851.

Keats, John. *John Keats: An Anthology*, Jarrold English Poets Series, Norwich: Jarrold Colour Publications, 1899.

Lang, Andrew. *The Pink Fairy Book*, London: Longmans, Green, and Co, 1897.

Lee, Seungyeon. "The Lightness of the Sexual Being: A Short Reflection on Hans Christian Andersen's "The Little Mermaid"", Societies, vol 8 (4), MDPI, Open Access Journal, pp1-5, November 2018.

Lewis, CS. *Till We Have Faces*, London: Geoffrey Bles 1956; repr. CS Lewis Signature Classics, London: William Collins, 2020.

Lönnrot, Elias. *The Kalevala*, tr. Keith Bosley, Oxford: OUP, 1999.

MacDonald, George. *Phantastes: A Faerie Romance for Men and Women*, London: Smith, Elder and Co, 1858; repr. New York: Ballantine, 1970.

Marie de France. *The Lais of Marie de France*, tr. Glyn S Burgess and Keith Busby, London: Penguin, 1986.

Mussies, Martine. "The Bisexual Mermaid: Andersen's fairy tale as an allegory of the biromantic sexual outsider." Presentation at the Third European Bisexual Conference, Amsterdam, 30 July 2016.

Ness, Mari. "Creating a Tale of Sisterhood: Snow-White and Rose-Red", *Tor.com* [online magazine], Tor Books/ Macmillan, tor.com, 25 January 2018.

Ott, Michael. "Wilgefortis", *The Catholic Encyclopaedia Vol. 15*, New York: Robert Appleton Company, 1912. newadvent.org/cathen/15622a, 3 April 2020.

Ovid. *Metamorphoses*, tr. David Raeburn, London: Penguin, 2004.

Petipa, Marius and Minkus, Ludwig. Ballet *Daughter of the Snows* (*Snegurochka*), premiered St Petersburg Imperial Bolshoi Kammeny Theatre, 19 January 1879; based on Alexander Ostrovsky's "The Snow Maiden" (1873), *Evropy Vestnik* 1878.

Pitman, Norman Hinsdale. *A Chinese Wonder Book*, New York: EP Dutton, 1919.

Pukui, Mary Kawena and Green, Laura (tr.). *Folktales of Hawai'i: He Mau Ka'ao Hawai'i*, Honolulu: Bishop Museum, 1995.

Ransome, Arthur. *Old Peter's Russian Tales*, London: Thomas Nelson and Sons, 1916.

Rimsky-Korsakov, Nikolay. Opera *The Snow Maiden*, St Petersburg Mariinsky Theatre, 29 January 1882, rev. 1898; libretto after Ostrovsky, (see above, Petipa); English tr. Brilliant Classics, brilliantclassics.com/ media/445955/94626-Rimsky-Korsakov-The-Snow-Maiden-Sung-texts-download-file.pdf: 2013.

Robey, David. *Sound and Metre in Italian Narrative Verse: an analytical database*. University of Reading, reading.ac.uk, April 2009.

Rosetti, Christina. "Goblin Market." 1862. Abrams, MH ed., *The Norton Anthology of English Literature 6th ed. Vol. 2*, New York: Norton, 1993.

Smith, Alexander McCall. *The Girl Who Married a Lion: And Other Tales from Africa*, Edinburgh: Cannongate Books, 2004.

Stahl, Caroline. *Fables, Tales and Stories for Children*, Nuremberg, 1816.

Tasso, Torquato. *Gerusalemme liberata*, 1587 ed. Carini, Anna Maria, Milan: Feltrinelli, 1961.

Tresidder, Megan. *The Language of Love: A Celebration of Love and Passion*, London: Duncan Baird, 2004.

Van Kampen, Claire, *Farinelli and the King*. London: Shakespeare's Globe Wanamaker Playhouse, 11 February–7 March 2015.

Wall, Josephine. Artwork *Psyche's Dream*, josephinewall.co.uk/artgallery/

Westervelt, WD. *Hawaiian Legends of Volcanoes*, Boston: GH Ellis Press, 1916.

Zipes, Jack ed., tr. *The Original Folk & Fairy Tales of the Brothers Grimm: The Complete First Edition*, Princeton: PUP, 2014.

Acknowledgements

This last year since the publication of *Asexual Fairy Tales* has been a life-changing one for me. I would like to thank all the readers and supporters who have taken this project to heart, especially those who have told me how much it means to them.

Thanks to everyone who has helped to get the word out, including AVEN (Asexual Visibility & Education Network), Folklore Thursday, the BBC We are Bradford project, BCB Community Radio, Brick Box, Origin Fine Foods, University of Huddersfield LGBTQ+ Society, Leeds LGBT+ Lit Fest, and everyone I have forgotten.

Thank you to SilverWood Books for all your hard work on the publishing front, the wonderful Swanwick Writers' Summer School (my writing family) and all the randomly encouraging people I've met online.

And lastly to all my family and friends for putting up with me and getting me through the bad times. I love you all.

Supporters

This book has been crowdfunded by Kickstarter. Many thanks to our generous supporters listed below and to those who choose to remain anonymous.

Laura Mantovani	Heather Osborne	Lena Marie Kjersem
Fen	Scarlett	Helen Lobel
Michelle Pessoa	Jamie	Cynthia Thompson
Erin Leigh Howard	Thor Erik Lie	Ariana Brady
Arthur Penndragon	Kaithecat9	Becca Keating
Sherri	Lauga	Kimberley Hoff
Ghislain Hivon	Sarah Kingdred	Demi Yeoh
Chelsea	Marcella van Diik	Lissalvy Tiegel
Cemre Esen	Kelly	Jeremy Drechsel
Nicole Ross	Meghan Thomas	Emma Smith
Serene Conneeley	Arpan Gupta	Charlye
Beth Stubenhofer	Kyra Matsuda	Aaron Bolyard
Adam Tolson	BunniesForTea	Guest 1714506549
Kaerien Yang	Kate	Alex Robnett
Amelia	Mark Sabellico	Jenifer Danes
Hannah Evans	Christie	Josefa Sandhill
Scarlett Jhanji	Beppo	Jessica
Jay Still	Natalie Doonanco	Mars Core
Emilie Wyqued	Sophia J Robinson	Jacob MacLeod
C	Erin Hartshorn	Sarah P
XJ	Natasha Liff	Kerenza
Malena	John Bankert	Lawrie
Cuddly Tiger	Julie Dick	Kathryn
Sarah Lippmann	Writingfanatic	M A Vespry
Le4ne	Sara	Brendon Eaker
Alison L	Ricky S	Daniele Bellavista
Emily Sargent	Lee	Han
Anna Cylkowski	Holly Holt	Dawn Carter

Linda Burke
JB Gordin
Courtney Dobbertin
Morven
Courtney Nash
Bonjuru
Dagmar
Danica Stone
Allie Carney
Alexa Donley
Caitlin
Sophia Hurd
Laura
Sarah Jackson
Joseph Inclan
Sarah Sketch
Guest 1020617965
Tomgeekery
Allie
Louise
Stiarna Askew
Jythie
Kuhla Shine
Treecakes
Briar
Stacey M
Allegra Tennis
Ladynightdeath
SMason
Audrey
Jessica Williams
Sarah Swafford
Harriet Nolan
Drew
Arinn Dembo
Peggy Griesinger
Sabrina Theobald

Brian Garcia
Alison Weaverdyck
Jeramie
Zeb Berryman
Kristine Kearney
Erica
Alexandra Long
Guest 1109124171
Mary Moore
Neil S
David Philip Norris
Helen Greetham
Michael Burgess
Whitney Chan
Michelle Cerullo
Jo Hornsey
Bettina Bergström
Indi
Mirva Lukkari
Rhiannon
Tanya
Corinne Foster
Sierra Randolph
Christine Gourley
Sydney
Danika
Birch
Áine O'Donoghue
Lowenna Penny
Desiree Thu Makowski
Brydon Caldwell
Lainey
Beatrice Berendonk
Melanie Davidson
Marni Sue
Mandy
Jonathan Middlemass

Colin-Roy Hunter
doodlerTM
Annelise Rue-Johns
Michèle Laframboise
Katy Thomes
Emma Johnson
Destinie Carbone
Sarah Beebe
Jae
Libby Midget-gem
Munnings
James Marsters
Emma Mullen
Susanreads
Aleta
Mendenhall-Turner
Ineffablelibrary
Rainbowbarf
Chchkiki
Andres D Bravo
Kat Henggeler
Oliver
Ellie
Lisa
Amanda
AndiKay
Eamonn Byrne
Joanne Lofthouse
Éliot Laquerre
Jessica Weinberger
Lucy
Lukáš Novák
Sarah Briggs
Fairy Hedgehog
Jérémie Pinguet
Vanessa
Stephroyer

Matt Trader
C
Wren Goldwin
Jaminx
Guest 1859869265
Matthew Clifford
Oliver Northwood
Kim Blanche
Becky
Anna Armstrong
Kezia-Rose Johnston
Heather Phelps
Jon Robertson
Chris Angelini
Anthony Pizzo
Devin
SuperDustin83
Alison Hommel
Smw116
Hannah Hazlehurst
Heather
Christopher J Gibson
PF Anderson
David J Bradley
Squidly1
Dre Lasana
Robynne Blume
Rachel
Robert Andrews
Stephanie
Jess Little
Kat Jansen
J Frank Beane
Elizabeth Winther
Benedict Patrick
T-Rose
S Chen

Brynn
Chrissey Harrison
Victoria Ford
Johanna Bracht
Camille Knepper
Marie
Tef Bannow
Rita McAuliffe
Lindsay Inskeep
Ja Racharaks
Rochelle Iambert
Keyana McAwesome
Carmen Finnigan
Maybeline Perey
Alma Seifer
Juliana White
Cat
Paul Kaefer
Julia Sutterfield
McKinney
Abigail Clark
Haeden Roswell
Kirsty Morgan
Olivia Montoya
Salvatore Puma
Hillary Froemel
Margaret Beatrous
Heather Esposito
Gina Boiardi
Guest 1471239395
Devinne Walters
Jessica Oehrlein
Katherine A
Anna Li
Kai Holmes
Sadie E Jeffries
Leslie

Alexa
Lluew Grey
Chey Saita
Maria Dorman
Ryan E
Jordan S
Cheryl Holland
Helen Louise Owen
Jamie Jack
Ida Umphers
Icy Oshawottz
Lora Wilson
Amanda Lewanski
Lea Mara
James Lucas
Patricia
Lisa Cavadias
Bailey Gorman
Samantha Carter
Amanda
Hangry-Bird
Jordan Schneider
Kimberley Lucia
Margaret Clark
Ally
Melissa
Savana Oberts
Helen Weldon
Edwin Mark Dakin
Daniel Clark
Leife Shallcross
Sophia
Bisignano-Vadino
Heather Valentine
Austin
Emily Metcalfe
Megan Krantz

Sarah

Claire Rosser

Neverwhere

Rachel Smith

Mariah Griffin

Dimitra Stathopoulos

Niki Turner

Jonathan Wager

Katy

Melanie Nazelrod

Amy

Pate McKissack

Mojosam

Jessica

Quinn Weller

Pyrrhalphis

Charis Papavassilis

Lauren Joy Moor

Jennifer Beltrame

Paul Trinies

Matthew Searle

Alycia Shedd

August Quinn

Filkferengi

Ruth Hult

Ernie Prang

Nina Brottman

Maria Tschakert

Eruvadhril

Valerie Kaplan

Danni

Keely Lawrence

Vida Cruz

Antti Hallamäki

Zoe

Lindsey Petrucci

Emily Hogarth

Mallory

Kari Holman

Cedar Skye Kilcrease

Beatrice Thirkettle

Holly Hamlyn-Harris

Emily

David Goodsell

Arioch Morningstar

Serpent_moon

Erika Sanderson

Rene

Kari Blocker

Ariel Button

Ezra Lee

Edith Olenius

Wil Bastion

Aren Bright

Thomas Bull

Ellen Howse

Drew G Jackson

Ernesto

Sia

The Creative Fund

Jess Turner

Paul Hiscock

Anna

Andy Yeoh

Kynerae

Lightning Source UK Ltd.
Milton Keynes UK
UKHW010108120522
402810UK00003B/60